IGNITING VENGEANCE

The Frost Fervor Concordance Book One

TOM HANSEN

IceBlazer
Entertainment

Igniting Vengeance

For all those with fire in their hearts.

When someone you love becomes a memory, the memory becomes a treasure.

— AUTHOR UNKNOWN

Prologue

Bone-chilling mist swirled about Imryll Farora as she stepped out of the Asternus Evocesco. Khatar stood by her side before she stumbled, his dexterous hands guiding the robe over her naked form. He buoyed her over to the frigid overlook of the Fellsstav Valley.

Frost-borne winds howled in the distance, filling her head with a comforting noise to drown out the raging torrent of the Concordance.

"It seems you had a good session, my Lady. I will prepare tea as soon as you are ready."

She needed a few seconds to regain her power and stand on her own, then the real work would begin.

"Another child has been born to the west." The words singed her tongue.

It could change everything.

Imryll's mind raced as she tied off her robe. So much to do before the vision fully dissipated. She had to verify. She needed to *know*.

"Is that the fourth child, my Lady? It's been years since the last one."

Her head stopped swirling as the rush of magic faded, and she took her first step. He bowed away as she steadied her weight on the corner of her desk.

Imryll narrowed her gaze to the desk overlooking Fellsstav Valley. Dark clouds converged overhead, bringing an endless winter to the frigid north.

Did the stars speak true, or deceive?

Her mind slowly churned as the images she'd seen in the trance coalesced into solid clues.

"Eight years."

She surveyed her desk, grabbing at papers and books, looking at their spines before tossing them away. Imryll took a tentative step, her legs still weak, but able to stand on her own. The beginnings of a plan formed in her mind.

"Eight years and eight days to be exact."

Khatar ground spices for the tea while she rooted and tossed. Ever so politely, he cleared his throat and indicated with his head at the pedestal. "A curious number, eight and eight."

Imryll gritted her teeth, resisting the urge to inflict pain on him for his insubordination. She had no time. She needed to look things up, she needed to find out what it all meant.

She dropped the book on the desk and flipped pages.

Imryll checked the first, then the second. It was an interesting start, but two do not a pattern make. Any number of things could have gone wrong in the birth, or the gestation period. Just because a child was born under a certain moon and star alignment didn't mean they'd been conceived under one.

She frowned when she checked the third. There was no

way a baby would have stayed in the womb that long, it would have taken a miracle, and some extremely rare components to make it work. Improbable.

But not impossible...

Imryll flipped pages in bulk to get closer, one page at a time. She didn't want to overshoot. She counted in her head, matching what she'd seen in the trance. She needed to be exact. After all this time, decades of clues could have led up to this final piece to the puzzle. She hoped it would end here. Her long search could be over.

Imryll's long blue fingernail slammed into the yellowed pages at the header. Her mind tried to comprehend the answer.

How could anyone know this?

She ran her fingernail down the first column, then back to the top of the page and halfway down the second column, looking for the right phase.

No, she didn't. She couldn't have.

Chills ran down her spine, starting from her forehead.

Imryll whispered the words to exit the Asternus Evocesco, ensuring she was no longer in the mystical trance. Any mistakes at this point would cost her more time, potentially decades.

She looked down at the page again, moving her finger down two more lines.

"But..." she trailed off, bewildered.

Imryll looked up where Khatar looked over a teapot. The aromas of honey and cinnamon filled the air.

"Get the sextant."

"My Lady?" He stopped when he noticed the fierce look in her eyes. "Oh...the sextant is right over—"

Khatar didn't merely walk across the room, he sprinted.

The coattail on his robe toppled the teapot. Cinnamon and rosehip powder flew into the air as the loose flame lit the small wood pile next to it.

She ignored his mistake. It didn't matter. Being this close to a breakthrough meant one needed to stay focused and not get distracted by minor annoyances.

Stepping to the window, she looked through the telescope.

Imryll scratched numbers onto a tablet, keeping one eye on the moon through the lens.

Khatar's fingers fumbled on the device.

She barked out numbers, he dialed them in.

"Got it." He didn't address her as My Lady this time, and she didn't care, she had seconds to get this figured out, or it would be years before they could test once more.

He placed the sextant in her hand. She pointed at the desk. "Second column, halfway down, third line after quarter constant."

His hands trembled as he looked for the mark.

"Thirty-four degrees, eighteen minutes."

Imryll looked through the sextant to confirm.

"Thirty-four eighteen."

She dropped the sextant, ignoring the hundred-year-old device as it cracked on the hard stone floor.

This was it. Double verified. A gift straight from the Gods.

Imryll looked up at her assistant, eyes wide.

"It's happened." Her lip quivered. "I can't believe after all these decades it's finally happened."

His face stricken, Khatar glanced at the small fire crawling up the tapestry in the corner.

Imryll snapped her fingers. With a chilling gust, the fire snuffed out, leaving behind a light dusting of snow.

"Shall...shall I inform The Translator?"

"Not yet. They haven't bloomed, and we are still years from a breakthrough. Much could still go wrong."

She sat down and looked across the frozen valley before her. The dark shimmer of the Feond just visible across the vast landscape.

A wicked smile spread across her lips. "Those children will be mine. Through them I will tear down the Feond and take my rightful place once again."

Imryll leaned forward, tapping her long fingernails on the rowan wood chair. "Oh yes, this is going to change everything."

Annoyance percolated in her mind. Why didn't she already have a cup of tea in her hand?

Chapter One

Steam roiled off Ynya Oblique's bare skin as she surfaced a few feet from her canoe. She wore a big smile on her thin face as she paddled the final few feet before climbing aboard.

"It only took me three days, but I got you!"

Behind her, a small wooden basket floated in the water. Inside, three lobsters snapped their bright red claws at each other as they tried to escape the surreptitious change in scenery.

Ynya watched the three jockey for position until her milky skin dried in the freezing mountain air. The cold never bothered her.

She glanced around, realizing how naked she was out here on the fjord lake.

Other than the light ripples across the surface from her own boat, nothing stirred on the cliffs or in the dark blue water.

"Of course there isn't anyone around, no one else would be so stupid to come out right now." She giggled as she kicked her feet in the water, enjoying the feel across her bare legs. She enjoyed this yearly trip. Alone is what she preferred. Alone worked best.

A quick glance through the ship's storage containers told Ynya everything she needed to know. Her small ship overflowed with fish! It would be enough to feed her family for months, even given the poor vegetable harvest this last season.

A muscle in her face twitched. At least she didn't have to travel down to Holmslatr. Her mother and father would make that trip soon.

"To see her."

Ynya stuck her tongue out at the thought. The old grievances needed to stay there, in the past. Worrying about bygones did nothing for the future. She would stay in Marsfjord and tend the garden and make sure Finny and Meki did their lessons.

Beneath her legs, a large cod came up to investigate the three lobsters in the basket.

She plunged her hand into the lake, grabbing the large fish right behind its gills. She pulled it from the lake, the cold water dripping off its scaly back, and brought it up to her face. "I'm sorry coddie, but you are going to be dinner for me."

Ynya focused her energy on her hand and into the fish. Steam poured off the fish and sublimated into the air around her. Within seconds the fish had stopped struggling and soon became rigid.

She relaxed her grip and dropped the cooked fish into her lap. After another quick glance around to make sure no one had followed her to watch her eat naked, she tore open the fish and scooped up the flesh with her hand, tossing it into her mouth.

Perfectly cooked and tasting amazing, Ynya wished she had brought some salt with her. That would have required planning, and planning wasn't exactly Ynya's strong suit.

Ynya finished off her meal and jumped into the lake to swim a few laps. The refreshing swim cleaned off the grease and bits of food caught in her hair.

She got back into the boat and stretched while the water steamed off her hot skin.

Ynya looked up at the sky. She felt safe nestled in here between the towering Razorclaws. The narrow field of view allowed her a small window to the heavens, and she wondered if the Gods Above watched her though that portal as she did in reverse.

After pulling in the lobster basket and stashing them with the others in the trolley behind the boat, Ynya tallied the fish. Twenty fish over her original plan meant she should begin the journey home.

The moon shone breathtakingly full tonight and would handily light her way through the fjord to home.

If she left now, she would make it home before the sun came up, possibly even surprise her family with a fresh cooked cod for breakfast.

Something bumped into her boat and she turned with a jump. A hunk of glacier ice bobbed in the water, just out of arm's reach.

"I suppose I should get dressed before I get home."

Her hair had already dried out by the time she got everything packed. She spent a few frustrating minutes trying to detangle her bright red curls before pulling the thin wool dress over her head.

Ynya's mother always made the dresses too big for her,

hoping she would fill them out at some point, but as she had told her mother every year since she could talk, "I'm never going to grow up or fill these out like you want, Mama. I'll always be your little girl."

She stared at the moccasins in the front of the boat and shook her head. Her Mama would never get it, would she? Even if she didn't, parents worried about their children regardless.

If only her mother had known the things Ynya had done. So many adventures, and so many close calls.

It was probably better for her mother not to know all the gory details.

Ynya grabbed the large oar, straddled the canoe with her bare feet, and paddled home, using the full moon to help her navigate her way through the hundreds of small ice chunks meandering across the lake's surface.

It had been a productive fishing trip, and Ynya's skin bristled with excitement to show her family the haul that would sustain them for the next few months.

Chapter Two

Ynya paddled all night to reach her hometown of Marsfjord, stopping twice to cook and eat more fish for energy.

The rising sun felt amazing on her skin as it came over the top of the buildings to the east.

Smoke already rose from various locations in the sleepy fishing village. A small haze hung over the town from the overnight fires.

Never having to stoke a fire for her own comfort, Ynya rarely thought about how different life was for the rest of the people in her town.

She had always been so independent that most people ignored her, which was fine by her. Ynya preferred the anonymity and freedom of not being beholden to the ways of life around her.

The smoke seemed too thick for such a calm morning. She expected a few fires, but these weren't localized in the dozens of chimneys around the village.

Something's wrong.

The acrid smoke hit her nose and she knew it wasn't simple wood fires to warm homes.

Entire homes had burned.

Panic welled in her chest and she quickened her paddling to get closer to the village at the end of the fjord.

"Mama, Papa!" Ynya yelled across the bay, knowing fully well they wouldn't be able to hear her from this distance. She didn't care, she cried out again.

Halfway across the bay, a small boat drifted lazily through the water. She rowed toward it, hailing to the figure in the vessel. "Hoi! Is something wrong in the village?"

No answer.

She paddled closer but stopped short when she saw into the boat.

It was her neighbor, Myrar. The middle-aged woman huddled over in the boat, three arrows her in her back. She wore only a nightdress. Even in the summer most people only wore such clothes to bed when they could be covered by skins and blankets. Had she tried to run in the middle of the night?

What is going on? Who could have done this? Marsfjord was a peaceful little fishing village that never bothered anyone.

Their boats drifted closer and bumped together. The woman's lifeless body didn't move, in fact, upon closer inspection, she was frozen solid.

Ynya's blood went ice-cold. If Myrar's body was frozen, she had to have been out here for at least a day. This didn't happen overnight, it had happened at least a day ago.

Ynya shuddered, almost dropping the oar in the water.

"Mama, Papa?" Her voice was barely audible in the stillness of the morning. Try as she might, she wasn't able to raise it higher than a whisper.

All around her, the sheer silence of the place tore at her mind. Now that the sun was high enough in the sky and not in her face, she saw the entire village clearly.

Ynya hadn't come home to a lively sea-side fishing village.

She came home to a graveyard.

The three dozen houses of her village of Marsfjord were all burned to the ground.

Two structures still smoldered, the larder house and the grain mill, most likely from the stores of food in them taking a couple days to fully burn.

Ynya's stomach roiled and she dropped to her knees, vomiting over the side and into the water.

She shuddered and heaved for a few minutes, until her stomach was empty. Her throat burned, and her eyes pained from the hot tears running down her cheek.

Ynya looked back up at the horrors laid out before her. Every single house was destroyed. Half a dozen bodies floated in the bay. Women and children, all in various states of dress, tossed out like chum. Some had arrows in them, others missed limbs. Many were burned, their pale skin blackened from the heat.

How many had been burned alive?

Her whole body twitched. She couldn't think, couldn't move. Part of her wanted to scream, another part wanted to cry, and yet another wanted to lash out in anger. Ynya remembered back to the lessons her mama had taught her about stress.

Calm your mind, take in data, process it one by one.

Above all, remove emotion and assess the situation as objectively as possible.

Ynya took in a shuddering breath, the cold air burning her lungs from the inside. She stood, straddling her boat and paddled forward.

With every stroke, Ynya focused her mind, focused her energy on a single spot in the village. Northern section, the mid-sized house with the glass structure behind it. Her mother's greenhouse, the only one in the village.

The glass was broken, scattered across the ground. Behind the broken glass the various green plants stood frozen in their growth.

Rage smoldered under Ynya's skin as she rowed closer and closer to Marsfjord. Occasionally, a body bumped against her boat, and she glanced down to ensure it wasn't someone she knew.

Isn't someone I know?

She laughed out loud, a psychotic, maniacal laugh. Of course, it was. Ynya knew everyone here. Surnames and given names for every last person cycled through her head.

The only ones she cared about, were the five at the top.

Mama, Papa, Synol, Finny, Meki.

Mama, Papa, Synol, Finny, Meki.

Mama, Papa, Synol, Finny, Meki.

The boat hit the wharf and Ynya stepped off like she'd done a thousand times before, she even grabbed the tie off rope and tossed it around the baluster.

Ynya paused, realizing what she had done. She'd just wasted time by tying off her boat.

She shook her head, trying to clear the haze.

Mama, Papa, Synol, Finny, Meki.

Ynya glanced into every home as she walked through the

village, counting the people she knew, looking at their faces, steeling herself for when she came across the place she dreaded, the one place she didn't want to go.

But she had to go. She had to know. Ynya couldn't turn away, she couldn't abandon them.

Regrets and what-ifs pummeled her thoughts, but she shoved them out. No time for those now.

Then she was there. She stood in the doorway and took in the horror.

Mama and Papa were dead.

Mama was just outside their family home. She lay on the ground, her dress pulled up above her head.

Papa lay just inside the house, his hand reaching out the door, his woodchopping axe buried deep in his back.

His axe, the one he chopped wood to warm his family, used to kill him?

Ynya stared at the horrifying scene, unable to process it, unable to move.

Then she heard a voice.

Chapter Three

"Ynya, my love."

It was her mother's voice. Ynya looked down, her emotions threatening to explode. There was no way her mother was still alive.

Ynya knelt, flattening down her mother's frozen dress to cover her exposed legs.

Tears welled in Ynya's eyes as she looked at her mother's still face. Her face was overly pale, and her matted red hair frozen to the snow, holding her in place. Blood splatters marred her perfect skin.

Numerous stab wounds to her mama's bare chest were simply too much to process.

"Mama?"

How is she still alive?

"Ynya."

She is alive!

Talia Oblique's white face looked back at her daughter. Pain sparked in her eyes, and Ynya knew she was not long for this world. How she had managed to survive out here in the cold for so long by herself, Ynya couldn't fathom.

Ynya fell to her knees and cupped her mother's face in her hands, pouring a gentle heat into them to warm her mother's cheeks.

"Mama, I'm here. Papa is dead–"

"I know." Talia's voice was weak and distant. It was small, like a flickering candle about to be snuffed out by an incoming gale.

"But Mama, where are the others, where are Finny and Meki?"

Talia's face winced at the mention of her daughters.

Ynya took the terror coursing through her head and focused it into a ball. She had no time for terror, she needed to somehow save her mother.

"I will warm you, Mama. I will get you to a cave so you can heal."

Ynya knew how to save her. Body heat, and if there was one thing Ynya was good at, it was body heat. She shrugged off her thin dress and built up heat under her skin.

"No, Ynya. Listen."

"But Mama–"

"They took your sisters. Finny and Meki, they are gone. Your father is dead, he had to watch, but he bled out two days ago."

Tears welled up in Ynya's eyes once again at the travesty of the whole situation. Two days? She's been lying here for two days?

"I can heal you Mama, then we can go find Finny and Meki."

Her mother coughed, a rough wheezing sound. Her

lungs had collapsed, and for the first time Ynya focused on the numerous stab wounds on her mother's chest.

Ynya needed to find a way to heal her dying mother.

Talia grunted, grabbing onto her daughter's arm and squeezing. "It's too late for me, my love. I waited, I held onto hope you would return. I must give you my power."

She coughed again, pink foamy blood bubbling from her mouth and oozing down her cheek.

Ynya used her dress to clean it off.

Her mother's magic had always been a mystery to everyone living in the village. Despite the mystery, no one could ignore all the good she did over the years. Talia healed ailments and mended broken bones. She tended crops, and even divined the best time for the fishing boats to leave and come home.

Some thought her able to control the weather when she needed to, to keep the fog at bay long enough for her husband's fishing vessel to make it home safe.

The Gods Above listened when Talia Oblique spoke, but she had never spoken about her powers before to Ynya.

"I'm here, Mama. What do you mean?"

"I held on long enough to see you one last time, so I can gift my power to you."

Her eyes glazed over as she looked past Ynya into the Void. They focused again and planted their blue gaze on Ynya's emerald eyes.

"Ynya, you must use this power to rescue your sisters. Promise me you will never stop. Promise me you will not leave anyone behind. You are all in danger. I should have prepared you better, I should have known this storm would darken our sky eventually."

Talia stared off at the Void again, her eyes glowing with a

dark and sinister light. Power built behind those eyes and Ynya felt the magic eddies surge around her mother's nearly-frozen body.

"Promise me you will rescue them all, don't leave any behind. Meki will be blooming soon and you need to be there before it happens. Keep them safe."

She looked off into the Void once again.

Questions on questions pulsed through Ynya's mind. What magic did her mother have? How would she transfer it? How was she still alive? How would Ynya use the magic? Where were her sisters?

Talia grunted, pulling her other arm from the frozen ground with a sickening icy crack.

Ynya's stomach flipped at the sound, imagining how painful that had to be for her mother. She should have been melting the ground around her mother. She should have gotten her somewhere safe. Talia was delirious, but she was still alive.

Talia grabbed Ynya's head, her rough hands surprisingly strong for a woman inches from death.

Power coursed through her mother's eyes. Only, they weren't her mother's eyes anymore. The blue was gone, replaced with a grey churning cloud. Shadow ringed her face and every contour of her thin, bony visage filled with twilight.

She was terrifying and beautiful at the same time.

"I'm so sorry, my little Ynya. You were never meant to have this burden. I never wished you to have to grow up. The Gods Below come for me, but the Gods Above look out for you."

Talia's eyes went wide.

Ynya's mind exploded with energy as power poured from

her mother's outstretched hands. Time seemed to stop all around them as her body filled with a new power. A dull, cold, throbbing heartbeat locked itself to hers. The magic thumped deep inside her chest, keeping a steady pace her heart struggled to match.

Her mother, now devoid of magic, crumpled to the ground, her lifeless arms flopping to the ground and her final breath exiting her lungs.

"Protect them."

The words were barely audible from her Mama's lips, but Ynya heard them as if she shouted.

Her mother passed on, all life leaving her eyes and face. Ynya knelt in the snow as an amalgamation of dread and rage pulsed inside her.

Chapter Four

Ynya didn't move for the longest time.

Her mother's lifeless corpse lay before her, her father's mere feet away, the blood from the axe wound in his back frozen like the rest of the village around her.

Her sisters had been taken.

Who has taken them? Where have they gone? Who is behind this?

She didn't have any answers, only more questions.

Ynya stood. Her mind still reeled from the events of the morning. She couldn't process that her mother had just given her magic. She was numb, confused, but mostly knew if she allowed herself to try to process those thoughts and emotions, she would become an emotional wreck.

Ynya needed to distract herself. She needed to take her mind off the trauma and focus on something productive.

Over the next few hours, she carefully melted her mother and father from their respective tombs and put them back into their own bed.

Ynya fell into the rote chores she always did. Before long,

she had all the fish from her haul brought in and stored safely in the icebox behind their home. They would be safe in there for months, but she hauled in some floating ice just to make sure.

For all she knew, her sisters would come over the rise from the road arm in arm singing with a handful of wild-flowers in their hands.

At least she hoped.

At one point, Ynya sat in their main room and cried. It was the only place in the entire town she felt she could finally allow her emotions to get the best of her. If she didn't release them now, in controlled outbursts, they would bottle up and come out at worse times.

Hot tears left painful marks across her face, a reminder of her duality in the frozen north. She was born of fire, but raised in frost. She had never belonged here, but Ynya had loved it. Her mother had made sure the skinny girl with red hair that melted ice with her feet fit in with the stoic northern fishing village.

When Talia married Ynya's father and moved here, she knew she had to earn the trust of the villagers, many who had never left the town their entire lives. Talia had done it by tending to everyone in the village.

Ynya had made the rounds hundreds of times with her mother.

She planted bulbs for the blind woman at the end of the row, the one who always smelled like day-old tobacco. They all called her Old Mam.

Ynya had never learned her real name, and now she never would.

Old Mam died in bed, her throat slit while she slept. At

least she hadn't had the indignity of being raped by the monsters who had killed everyone.

A shudder went through Ynya once again as she thought about her mother. How she had held on to life for days, waiting, hoping her daughter would come back home.

The thought led to dark place in Ynya's mind. Thoughts swirled through her head.

What if I had come home a day later, or a day earlier? What if I had never left at all?

She wished she hadn't left, at least she wouldn't be left here suffering while everyone else was dead.

No!

Those thoughts had no room here. This was a somber day in a remorseful town. This was now a place where the dead would rest. They deserved it.

Ynya followed her mother's example and served her people the only way she could. She went through the entire town placing people back in their beds, thawing them enough to get their bodies into peaceful positions.

She unmoored the boat and took it out into the bay, collecting the dozen bodies floating there.

She matched babies with mothers, sons with fathers, husbands with wives, and laid everyone to rest back in their own homes, where they would be safe.

It was warm where they lay. Warm and safe and with each other and the Gods Above and Gods Below.

And when Ynya was done, she sat in her family's home once again, covering up her parents with their furs and blankets.

Ynya listened once again to the cold heartbeat inside her. That hard, frigid place had lived inside of her mother for all these years. She supposed for anyone but her, cold was a way of life.

Ynya barely knew the cold, even though she had grown up in it, she had never fully experienced it like those dead around her, like her sisters had.

She carried a steady reminder of how the rest of her family lived, strumming inside her chest.

For a while, she searched within her, unable to understand how her mother's magic worked, but she soon abandoned the quest.

It was too soon. It was too soon to make the magic her own. The power was too much like her mother, caring and thoughtful; always planning.

Eventually, the cold thump became colder, icy, and her own heart beat faster, filling her chest with an intense heat.

Anger stirred within her.

No, it was fury. Someone had come, and in one brutal swipe, taken everything from her. Ynya was now alone with a shard of ice deep within her fiery heart.

The heat grew and grew, stoking the fires of rage and revenge.

Her mother asked Ynya to find her sisters, and she would.

For a moment, she wondered if Synol had been taken, but Synol was with new her husband, in a town to the south.

It was Finny and little Meki, her two younger sisters, who Mama had asked her to find.

"I will find them."

Ynya balled her fists as she stood over her mother. "I will find your daughters and I will keep them safe for you, Mama. I will make those that have harmed you pay for what they have done."

Rage continued to build inside her. Ynya shook with the immense heat in her head. The roots of her hair glowed, bathing the small room in a brilliant white light as the sun set behind her.

Inside her, the heat and cold warred, each attempting to win an unseen battle, but heat and rage won. She would figure out her mother's magic another day. She pulled out a dozen frozen fish from the icebox and cooked four. She lost an entire day here at the village. She wondered if she should have left immediately to hunt down her sisters, but in her heart, she knew respect for the dead in her village would grant her protection for what was to come.

She prayed to the Gods Above and the Gods Below to grant her strength in her quest. She prayed for her sister's safety and swift resolution to the nightmare that tore her family apart.

"I am coming Finny. I am coming Meki. Synol, I will come for you too, for Mama told me to collect all my sisters and keep you safe."

Chapter Five

As the moon came up behind her, Ynya left the village heading east.

Marsfjord was a small coastal village nestled along a rocky beach of the Razorclaws, but there was not a main road leading through it. Instead, the road sat atop a small rise overlooking the whole area, like the ground had shifted upwards as you went more inland.

Ynya turned once she reached the road, looking for a time over her birth place. It might be the last time she saw it and she wanted to set it to memory.

It was peaceful now, with only couple smoldering fires Ynya extinguished. The town slept. Now, Gods willing, they would all find rest from the violence that had beset them.

She turned and found herself on the ruts of the Hyndalskyr road. It ran north and south through the entire district. It was at this point Ynya realized she had never taken this road anywhere in her life.

It was early spring here in the far north, which meant rain, mud, and the occasional snow flurry. There were also no fresh tracks leading south other than the occasional solo mule with boot prints from a fisherman going to Holmslatr to sell his catch.

Those tracks leading south weren't the issue. The tracks leading east to Lyraville however, were deep and wide, meaning a larger contingent of people came through here not long ago.

Ynya turned south and looked out over the endless white and brown. When Synol got married six months ago, she had to travel this road. She had left her safe family town in the dead of winter during a blizzard in order to reach her groom's family in a harbor town to the south.

It was the last time anyone saw Synol.

Ynya's mother had waited patiently for spring to come so she could go visit her daughter. She was supposed to head south in a few days' time.

As soon as I got back from my fishing trip.

Ynya almost lost herself to her emotions once again, but she steeled herself from the overwhelming emotions and dug her fingernails into the fleshy part of her hands. The pain reminded her why she was here. It reminded her of her commitment. She wouldn't just run away this time.

"You can't just run away when you have responsibilities, Ynya." Echoes of Synol's arguments bounced inside her mind.

"But you ran away from our family, Synol. You are not here right now. I'm here, and I have to clean up the mess."

Steam rose from below her, and she looked down at her fingernails, beginning to glow red hot from the anger welling up inside her.

A wicked smile crossed Ynya's lips. "I will clean it all up."

She headed north, following the most recent tracks leading into Marsfjord.

Half a mile up the road, she turned to face east. This was the furthest she'd ever been away from Marsfjord on the east side. She'd been all over the fjords, ice caves, and inlets to the west. Ynya knew more about the Razorclaw Fjords than anyone else in town, but she'd never come farther east than the road.

Gritting her teeth, she stepped past the invisible line in her head, and continued down the silent road.

Along the way, she tried to take in as much as she could about the terrain, the road, and its conditions.

Boot prints, horse prints, and wagon ruts abounded in the mud, which meant they were organized. Officers and lackeys both came along this road.

A recently broken wheel discarded to the side meant they had traveled with a wagon, possibly two.

Still, Ynya only found enough evidence to suggest there was one wagon, and it was a big one. It would have been loaded down with a lot of provisions for the journey because the ruts it left were deep in the hard-packed clay.

Or it carried people.

Ynya'd been through her entire village. The three people she didn't find and place back in their homes for rest were her two younger sisters, and Hvarf, a kindly older gentleman whose wife had died three winters back. He had left for Holmslatr to sell his wares the same day Ynya left for her fishing trip.

I hope he's still alive.

Ynya continued along the eastbound road all night, stopping once to cook and eat another fish.

Every crackle of bone and slurp of mouth reverberated in

her head more than normal. She was the loudest thing out here and the eerie silence terrified her more than the tracks in the snow.

Ynya buried the fish bones under the soil, and dusted her small temporary camp in powder, suddenly aware how alone she was right now.

Wasn't solitude what she had been relishing just a day or two before? How quickly priorities changed when your world shifted beneath your understanding.

Ynya spent time scrutinizing the road ahead. She tried to memorize every track, print, and divot in the muddy soil. She noted the hoof prints from the horses, three of them. One larger and heavier than the rest, with two others tied to the wagon, their prints overwritten by the wheels.

Then there were the foot soldiers. Their prints were haphazard and scattered, like the men had been marched for so long they couldn't follow a straight line. The rut they followed was deep but only as wide as a man's shoulders. They had to have been following along in single file for them to be making such a track.

But the most curious ones she found were prints outside the convoy, a single person wearing moccasins. Every step had been planned, and meticulously placed in the soft tundra. Whoever made them walked with surety, like they had been trained to walk through snow and barely leave any tracks.

They never faltered, never broke more ground than was needed for a single footstep, and never turned to the side or backed up. In fact, if a storm had come through and dusted these footprints with even the slightest snowfall, Ynya would have never seen them.

Those footprints terrified her the most. Whoever made them knew what they were doing.

Something crunched in the distance, the soft sound of the thin crust of the melting snow breaking. It was followed by a deeper sound as the weight hit the heavier snow beneath. It was a distinct sound that Ynya had heard a thousand times in her childhood while she played hide and seek.

A footstep.

Chapter Six

Ynya crouched to the ground and listened.

She was glad she had the moon's light to guide her and hadn't done something so stupid like use her hair to light her way.

But she had been so focused on the ground in front, studying the tracks and footprints, she had forgotten she was tracking a band of murderers and rapists.

She needed to be more careful. She couldn't risk getting her sisters killed by her own stupidity. Talia would never forgive her.

Remembering her mother, Ynya felt for the cold heartbeat in time with her own. It was still there, an enigma waiting to be unlocked, but now wasn't the time for testing of a newfound magic skill, now was the time for caution.

Ynya was exposed here on the small rise. She moved to the side about thirty paces before poking her head above the hill to look out on the valley below.

There were men, about a dozen if her eyes didn't deceive her. Some stood and stretched, but most of them sat on the packed earth, drinking from skins and chatting with their neighbors.

At first, panic rose through her body as she counted them out.

How am I going to take on twelve men by myself?

She realized there was no wagon.

Her heart beat faster and she counted them all again. Eleven men, but no one else. No smaller fire-headed girls among them.

This was good news. They didn't have her sisters.

All the men wore traditional parkas and boots for living and working in the north. Most likely from Lyraville or somewhere in the Hyndalskyr, these appeared to be her people. Normally seeing someone dressed like this wouldn't give Ynya any reason to think they were enemies.

Only she had never known this many men to be traveling out in the nighttime along a road rarely ever used during the day.

These men shouldn't be here, and that meant they were up to no good.

After a few minutes, one of them barked orders, rousing the remaining men into action.

Slowly, the men formed into a loose line and continued to trudge through the snow westward toward Marsfjord.

A sharp worry swept through Ynya's body.

They're patrolling the road between the two towns!

Had she stayed in Marsfjord for one more day, the soldiers would have found her while she milled around her burned out hometown. She would have been taken prisoner like her sisters.

Ynya frowned.

What happened that would cause a group of men to travel between towns like this?

They left, trudging through the snow. Every so often one of them would trip, falling into the man in front of him. They would recover while the man in front barked epithets at them before continuing on.

Ynya realized why one of the tracks she'd been studying was so erratic. These men had no idea how to walk in snow! They must have been brought up from somewhere farther to the south and given northern clothes to blend in, but knowing how to live in the north was a skill you acquired over time. Most of these men were not of the north.

But one of them was. The leader knew how to walk in the snow. Each footstep was solid and sure.

Ynya thought back to the lighter separate footprints from earlier. Despite knowing how to walk through the deeper northern snows, he was still too large, and there was no way he could walk across the tundra while making such small footprints.

A bitter smile crossed her face.

They had to have been there for the ransacking and murder of her village, these men clearly had been part of it, and they would know where her sisters were. If these men weren't used to the cold north, then maybe her fire would surprise them, possibly hurt one of them until they gave up the information she sought.

Ynya thought about running in, grabbing one of them and dragging him off, but no, that wouldn't be a good idea.

The immediate area had no trees or large rocky outcroppings. It was flat with little contour to the frozen landscape. With half a mile between rises, there was nowhere to hide for long.

"Dammit." Ynya said under her breath. "I will be back for you."

She would. She would mete out revenge on every person who wronged her family and her town.

These men, all of them, would die by her hand.

Reluctantly, Ynya pulled away from the small hill and skirted around the soldiers, putting some distance between the group and her back. After a while, she watched them in the distance starting to crest the small hill she'd just come over.

"I will be back."

"But you never went anywhere," a woman's voice replied.

Panic rose in her chest as Ynya whirled around looking for the source. A female soldier explained the footprints being so light.

A white flurry blinded Ynya and something struck her on her head, knocking her down.

Ynya's heartbeat raced as pain lanced through her skull. She rolled backwards, trying to keep a view on her attacker, but all she saw was blackness and white flurries.

From her side came the voice again, this time closer. "So thin."

Something wrapped around Ynya, blacking out all her vision. "I've been watching you for a while, little one. You are a feisty one, aren't you? What are you doing out so late?"

The force that wrapped around Ynya flipped her upside down into something large – a sack perhaps? Ynya flared her magic for a second, about to burn her way out from her prison, but the cold beside her heart snuffed out the heat she grasped.

Patience, my love. Give it time.

Her mother's voice echoed through Ynya like a ghost. She stopped struggling, stopped moving and listened, but the voice never came again.

Ynya flared her fire once again, but then changed her mind. Her mother had told her to be patient. Maybe she should listen.

She dropped her magic, rage still coursing through her veins just under the surface.

Ynya would wait, she would listen, and she would watch.

And then, she would strike and make them all pay.

Chapter Seven

"Look at what I caught here, boys!"

Ynya hit the ground hard, bounced, and came to a rest another foot away. Her head hit the icy terrain first, then her shoulder, shooting pain down her back. She should have turned over in the sack.

"What is it?"

The sack opened, and someone grabbed Ynya by the hair and pulled her upright.

"Found her snooping around behind us."

The woman had her hands in Ynya's long wavy hair, yanking her around to show her off to the men.

Salacious looks crossed their faces as they took her in.

"Sweet morsel."

"Come to give us a present?"

"Hope she's feisty as you are."

The woman threw Ynya back to the ground, and then moving like the wind, she knocked down three of the men in a flash. Ynya got a good look at her attacker and realized why she hadn't been able to see the woman.

She's covered head to toe in white fur, like a frost bear!

It made her near-invisible in the light flurries and black backdrop of the starry sky.

All the woman had to do was stop moving, maybe crouch down, and Ynya would have walked past her without even noticing her. The whole thing would've been especially easy since Ynya had been watching the soldiers and not the ground.

Ynya needed to be more careful next time, but the more pressing matter was to get herself out of this situation.

Something glinted in the moonlight, and a thin silver blade appeared next to the throat of the last man to hit the ground.

"Care to continue your line of thinking, Hans?" The woman's blade stopped right under his ear, digging into his skin just enough that blood welled, coating the tip of the blade and dripping onto the snow with each of his labored breaths.

She pulled the man's furry hood back, exposing his darker skin and deep eyes. He trembled.

"No, ma'am. Didn't mean nothing by it."

"Didn't think so." She dropped him, spun her blade around in her hand, and was about to put it back into some hidden sheath when she noticed the blood on the tip.

The man who had been leading the other men spoke up for the first time. "Kalda."

His voice was deep and rich with wisdom. His tone was calm, meaning he'd probably spent a lifetime waiting on people to follow orders. He wasn't a man who had to yell. He spoke and people obeyed.

Kalda flashed him a fierce scowl, and stormed off into the

snow, grumbling under her breath about southern men and blood staining her blade.

"You three. Continue with the group while I interview our little rapscallion here." The man bent down and extended a hand to Ynya.

For a second, she thought about burning the man where he stood. He was the only competent one in the party besides Kalda, and harming him would give her enough time to run for it. She glanced out into the snow to look for Kalda, but the woman was already lost in the darkness and snowfall.

Ynya realized she'd blown her one chance to escape, and it would probably be prudent to play the role of someone lost in the snow, rather than someone on the hunt.

She took the hand and stood. "I'm from Lyraville, and I got lost in the snow."

"Lyraville, eh? That's at least five miles from here, how did you manage through the snow without any clothes?" He looked her up and down, and she suddenly realized just how bad this looked. She normally never wore anything more than this due to her own internal magic heat, but to outsiders, people who hadn't spent time with her, they wouldn't easily comprehend how she could survive in the frozen north.

She needed a plausible lie.

"I had just dug myself a burrow in the snow to sleep in when she came and grabbed me. My stuff is still out there now."

It wasn't a complete lie. Ynya did have a pack out in the snow somewhere, and for all they knew she was just bunking down for the night. Snow caves were so well-insulated once you crawled into them that most people shed their outdoor clothes for the warmth of the cramped space.

He scrutinized her for a moment, his bushy eyebrows furrowing with worry and concern. He could be a nice man if he wasn't leading a group of murderers.

Ynya meted out her breaths, hoping he took the bait.

"Lyraville's been taken over by my soldiers for weeks now. How have you survived this long by yourself?"

He squatted down, concern on his face. He didn't believe her.

"I've patrolled this stretch of road for two weeks now and I haven't seen anyone come by here. If you've been out here this whole time we would have seen you."

He reached out his hand and grabbed Ynya by the wrist. Shock hit his eyes as he felt her hot skin. For a half moment he was confused by the sudden warmth, but she didn't wait.

Ynya poured a massive amount of heat into her wrist, just below the surface of her skin. The patch under his hand glowed a faint white in the darkness.

He glanced over his shoulder at his men. "Hey! Bring the chains! I think they're going to want to see this one."

In between calm heartbeats, Ynya pushed the heat from her wrist into his hand.

He let go, his eyes wide with alarm.

The pungent scent of burning flesh filled the air as Ynya whirled around and took off running into the night. She'd managed to burn him far worse than she thought.

She was a dozen yards away before his yell hit her ears, but Ynya kept running, kept zig-zagging through the snow.

She couldn't go back to her pack, and she couldn't get caught by the woman in white again. She needed to keep running to stay out of reach.

Before long, she stopped, and crouched down in the snow.

Ynya surveyed every inch of the horizon around her. Nothing. Not a hare, not a moose, not a single woman wearing a bear's skin.

She'd made it, somehow.

The Gods Below had helped her escape and she would not put that grace to waste again.

Chapter Eight

Ynya spent the rest of the night trying to get back to her pack, but every time she came within sight of it, she noticed a prowling Kalda.

Kalda was good, too. She staying far enough away from Ynya's pack that it wasn't always obvious she was nearby. But she stayed close enough to easily catch Ynya.

Dammit, I'm going to have to leave it behind. I'm so stupid.

Not watching where she was going, and not paying attention to her surroundings had lost her food and weapons tucked in the pack. The handful of knives she'd brought with her for gutting fish were all she had taken before leaving the town. Even though they might not have been soldier-quality, they were sharp.

But they weren't effective in the slightest if she didn't have them on her.

After long last, the sun started to come up and Ynya realized this was a futile effort. She'd wasted too much time trying to get back to her pack.

Realization dawned on her more as she followed the road eastward once again. Every mile or so, another soldier monitored their spot, vigilantly surveying the land to the north and south..

Ynya'd spent so much time trying to get back to her pack she'd given all the soldiers plenty of time to fan out.

Ynya couldn't follow the road anymore.

She had reached the Skoroberg, a massive, sheer wall of solid rock jutting hundreds of feet into the eastern sky.

Much like the shorn terrain that separated her town of Marsfjord from the road, another, much larger step in the land separated the district of Hyndalskyr from Skoro.

Nestled at the base of the Skoroberg was Lyraville, a small town about twice the size of Marsfjord functioned as a stop-off point before travelers ventured up the rocky berg to get to Skoro.

The town crawled with soldiers. By the time Ynya'd gotten within sight of the massive cliff of rock, soldiers had spread out along the base, preventing her from even reaching the rock.

A single road wound up through the rock with narrow, steep switchbacks, the only passage from the bottom to the top for miles in each direction.

Even though she'd never been this far east, she'd heard stories from her father about the area many times. The vast cliff disappeared over the horizon in the distance, something Ynya hadn't believed until she saw it with her own eyes. If she couldn't make it up the road, her only option was to scale the wall, leaving herself exposed and vulnerable on the rock face, assuming she could even make it up on her own.

She was stuck.

Proceeding forward meant capture, and the ever-vigilant

eyes of the soldiers scanning the area around the road meant they had her cornered.

Ynya didn't know where her other two sisters had been taken, and there was no way she was going to be able to get past this blockade.

She needed to get on the south side of them. She needed—

No. I don't want to go there. I don't want to see her.

Ynya sighed.

She needed to go back. Two sisters were inaccessible, but one would be just to the south.

"Synol."

Even saying her sister's name dredged up years of bad memories. The constant fighting, the endless bickering. Best friends in childhood eventually turning into mortal enemies the last few years.

Ever since I Bloomed.

Ynya had celebrated when Synol finally left, the family no longer fought as much as they did when she was around.

She had one choice; to return back to Marsfjord and proceed south. She had to find her older sister who lived in her new town with her new husband.

Ynya slept most of the day, since movement on the plains in the sunlight was too risky.

When night fell, she ran like the wind, veering far north until the terrain changed. She jogged along the start of the Razorclaws where the smaller hills and rocky terrain hid her movements and were far enough from the road that single soldiers wouldn't ever see her.

She traveled all night long, finding herself back in Marsfjord before the sun came up.

She was famished and dehydrated. Hours of running,

combined with her usual hot metabolism, drained her of energy. By the time she got back to the tomb that was her town, her stomach pained, her legs ached, and she had developed a massive headache from the lack of food.

A quick survey told her the soldiers hadn't come this far west. She'd been smart telling them she was from Lyraville, and it was fortuitous she'd been caught on the eastern side of their position. They had no reason to doubt she was trying to get back to her hometown, or at least hover close to it in hopes the soldiers left.

She cooked and ate five fish, then dug into the unburned portion of the town larder for grain and fats. There was some wilted spinach she fried up with pig fat for a tasty snack.

Before leaving, she stopped by her house once more to check on her parents.

"I don't know how well she's going to accept me, Mama. I don't know if she'll turn me away, but I promise I will not stop, I will not quit until all my sisters are safe."

She watched her parents in their eternal slumber for a while, then reverently walked up to them and removed the obsidian necklace from her mother's neck, and the obsidian ring from her father's frozen finger.

They wouldn't be needing them anymore, and she wanted something to remember them by. It also might come in handy to show Synol to convince her something had happened to their parents.

Ynya had never seen their parents without these marriage trinkets, and they looked like strangers to her without them.

They look like strangers because they are dead and frozen.

Neither of them had much to call their own, other than two boats, fishing tools and those pieces of jewelry.

Ynya clutched the two tight in her fist. Then she donned both the necklace and ring, having to put the ring on her thumb so it wouldn't fall off. She said goodbye once again to her mother and father.

"I will not return without her, I promise."

Chapter Nine

✥

The road leading south through Hyndalskyr ended up being patrolled as well.

What has changed so drastically in the world to warrant such a change in this tiny northern berg?

Sixteen years Ynya had lived here, with nothing out of the ordinary happening. Sixteen years of fishing, of brutal winters and mild summers.

Sixteen years of playing with her sisters, of exploring the Razorclaws with Synol whining about going back before sundown. Sixteen years of Ynya pushing her sister to lighten up.

Now it had all changed in three short days. Three days of fishing, out in the middle of nowhere, far from anyone.

Ynya thought she wanted time alone, and now she had it.

She had too much of it.

Ynya stayed far enough away from the patrols on the road to avoid being seen, while also keeping them close enough to know where each one was.

These were the dumb soldiers, the idiots who clomped

through the terrain haphazardly. They were not used to the crunch of the snow, or the bite of the wind. None of them were from around here and their presence only brought up more questions.

Why, after sixteen years of growing up around people who know my every strand of hair, can I not find a single other northerner?

The going south was painfully slow. The endless patrols veered farther away from the road now, probably because they had been notified of her presence.

They were just not as good as Ynya. While she had never been down this road personally, she grew up in this area. She knew nothing else, nothing but the snow and the blinding white.

She was also able to traverse the terrain without the bulky clothes of a northerner. At night, Ynya found better comfort out under the stars by melting through the snow and ice to get to the hard packed earth underneath. Packing herself in insulating snow like anyone else would do, was too warm for her.

While back at Marsfjord, she had donned a white dress, allowing her to blend into the background better. Now, her hair was the only thing to give her away as her milky white skin blended into the snow along with the dress.

But the hair didn't become a problem as she allowed the snow to pile in it.

Don't melt the snow and it will do well to hide my locks.

As she made her way, something stood out to Ynya in the otherwise thin snow. A horse-sized pile that didn't belong there.

Panic welled in her chest, but she forced it down, willing her heart to slow as she assessed the situation. Despite the danger, Ynya felt compelled to check what was under the pile. She needed to know.

Once sure the woman in white was nowhere in sight, Ynya crept through the snow. Her heart pounded in her chest as she poked through the upper layer to a hard, frozen block of ice below.

Frost fell away, betraying the leathers and furs beneath.

It was a human.

Her heart sank as she took in the aged leathery face and wide flushed red nose of a man she knew.

It was Hvarf, and his mule.

It didn't take her long to uncover enough to find out what had killed him either. An arrow to the heart pierced his back and lodged itself into the ground under him. It was an accurate and deadly hit.

The arrow was finely made, and running her finger along the shaft, Ynya realized she was not dealing with the amateur soldiers here. The black arrow was straighter than anything Ynya had ever seen in her life. The shaft was a dark hardwood, shaved and polished with such care she saw the reflection of the stars in it.

She'd been around expert marksmen before. Synol had been rather adept with a bow, since she never took to the water like Ynya had. Synol's fletching had to make do with pieces of driftwood, or the scraggly pines dotting the land to fletch her arrows. She'd never had any wood this straight before.

"Hey!" A man's voice rang out in the distance.

"Shit!" She swore to herself.

Studying an arrow so closely she allowed another one of the stupid patrols to sneak up on her once again.

Something whistled through the air, striking her legs as she stood to run.

Metal bands clapped about her ankles, binding deep into her flesh and wrapping themselves around her ankles twice.

Her forward momentum and tied-together feet threw her into the snow face-first.

She forced immense heat into her ankles, to melt up the caltrops.

She was glad she wore a thin white dress. It would distract the soldier long enough to keep him from seeing the red-hot metal around her ankles.

Come here you bastard.

"Well, well, what do we have here? Oh look at you!"

The man loomed over her, taking in every inch of her. She twisted and struggled, but only ended up flopping over to her back.

His eyes went wide as she did it, and his jaw fell open for a moment.

She poured more heat into her bindings, and smiled at him. Anything to keep him distracted and looking up.

"I'm lost."

His slack-jawed expression turned to one of lust and he began to scan down her body once again. The chains were glowing now, and would soon melt, but she needed more time.

"They sent me out here for you."

His eyebrows raised. "They did, huh? Good taste."

"Well?" She asked, trying to keep the terror in her voice from breaking her concentration. "You going to undress?"

He undressed much faster than she thought, but it was too late by the time he had his pants off.

Her chains had softened enough to pull apart. As soon as

her legs were freed, Ynya flung the molten metal at the man, catching him in the gut. It seared through his skin, burning into his stomach, and lodged in his flesh as his body absorbed the heat of the metal.

Surprisingly, the man didn't scream. He looked down at the smoke and steam coming out of his bare stomach like he couldn't quite believe what had just transpired. He fell to his knees as he clutched his stomach and stared up at her with a surprised expression.

She was up and behind him, putting him into to a choke hold. Heat poured off her forearms as she choked him to the point of exhaustion.

Soon, he slumped to the ground, his body limp. The smell of cooked flesh singed her nostrils.

Ynya's lip quivered as her brain came back into control.

I just killed a man!

But I had to!

Ynya scrambled away backwards. Away from the last member of her village, away from his frozen mule, and away from the soldier who had stumbled across her.

She sat there for a long minute, willing her mind to slow down. Ynya's heart thundered in her chest as she did everything to avoid looking at the ghastly sight before her.

Her heart eventually calmed to a semi-peaceful rate.

She realized she was right off the road, and visible to patrolling soldiers. Hvarf and his mule wouldn't raise any suspicions, other than his body now uncovered, but the sentry man would.

Begrudgingly, Ynya grabbed the man and tugged him farther away from the road, dragging him through the snow along with her pack.

She then went back over the area and smoothed out the

snow well enough to throw off any casual observer. Ynya couldn't risk anyone investigating and discovering his body. They would know she went this way, and would most likely discover her plans of heading south.

After dragging him over the hill, Ynya heard another voice over the distance. It was barely audible over the wind, but it came from the road.

"Oi, Grof, where you go? Time for shift change!"

Chapter Ten

"Grof? Where you—oi, there you are! You deaf, man?"

Ynya stood at the top of the small rise, fully dressed in the dead man's bulky skins. She faced away from the man coming up from behind her. Directly beneath her, just past the peak in the hill, was the man she'd stolen the clothes from, the man she'd gutted with his own red-hot chains.

Apparently, his name was Grof, and it was a good thing he was skinny like her or his clothes wouldn't have fit.

Ynya felt sick to her stomach. She still hadn't fully gotten over the fact that she'd just killed a man with her magic.

To make things worse, she'd stolen his clothes and they smelled awful.

The man behind her chuckled. "Eh? You taking a whiz there? You better put your pecker away before it freezes off, ya know!"

Whiz? Oh!

She finally got what he was talking about. She raised her hand behind her to indicate he was correct.

"Well hurry up, we're freezing our asses off out here."

"Oi! You find him?" Another voice wafted in from behind.

"Tell him to stop pissing in the snow and come in for a pint. He's buying the first round for making us all wait this long!" This was from a new voice.

Ynya groaned inwardly.

Now there were three guards. If it had been one, she would be able to take him, at least that's what she'd hoped by donning the first guard's clothes. But with two more at the road, if she killed the one, at least one would run back and tell the others.

The soldiers would know where Ynya was, and she couldn't have that.

Bundled up in these clothes, she was practically invisible. Her only exposed skin was through a narrow hole in her hood, and even her eyes were so surrounded by bushy fur she doubted anyone would notice.

Now, she just needed to play along.

Ynya didn't know enough about male anatomy to convince them she was peeing in the snow, but she bounced up and down and shook her leg like she'd seen some of the men do off the side of the boat.

"Well throw me out into the cold, he's finally done. Next time don't drink so much before patrol, mate."

Soon, Ynya had a couple manly arms over her shoulders and the four of them made their way back down the road.

Luckily, she never had to say a word because her three compatriots never seemed to stop talking.

"So, Capt says there is a girl out there, you hear? Supposed to be wearing naught but a shift in the snow, so I says to him, why don't you look twenty feet away from where you lost her? That's as far as she got."

This got an uproarious laugh from the others. Ynya tried to laugh, but got slapped on the back so hard and so unexpectedly she almost stumbled to the ground.

Her anger flared, preparing to retaliate from the attack, but the laughing continued. She reminded herself that men interacted different with each other than women.

Do I need to insult them to be one of them?

She didn't even know any insults that would hurt anyone's feelings. What about her voice?

Ynya shrugged it off. Better to remain silent while these morons prattle on about nothing at all.

And they say women are the chatty ones.

The biggest issue was all the heat she generated while angry. Walking the couple miles back to the encampment didn't help. Ynya was beginning to overheat, and she needed to take her hood off to let the pent-up energy escape.

Only she couldn't give away her identity.

Why am I coming into their camp? This might be the stupidest decision I've made up to this point.

The camp wasn't huge, but a dozen tents were laid out in a circle around a larger tent in the center, most likely a mess tent. One of the surrounding tents in the back was larger than the others.

A guard stopped the four as they came into the camp and asked them to give status updates. The three men before Ynya gave theirs; nothing, nothing, and a whole lot of nothing.

Then the soldier looked at her.

Oh no! She would have to talk. Ynya readied her gruffest

sounding voice, when one of her companions elbowed her hard in her chest.

Ow! Her temper flared once again.

"This one's been doing nothing but pissing in the wind. Yellow snow and all."

The guard asking the questions paused, looked up, and narrowed his eyes at Ynya. "That boring?"

She nodded, trying to keep her rage from showing. Her breast stung from the blow, and tears of pain filled her eyes. As much as she wanted to burn her 'friend' right where he stood, she was grateful his manly antics negated her need to talk.

After the guard let them go, the four came to the big tent.

The man who had elbowed Ynya in her chest slapped her on her back once again. "I told you, first rounds on old Grof here, right?"

She grunted, and fumbled around on her belt for a coin purse she'd felt when putting on the clothes.

Ynya weighed it in her hand, then tossed it in the air. "On me!" She said in the gruffest voice she could.

The money pouch distracted the men so much that they didn't notice how she spoke. One of them grabbed it and turned to head into the tent. As he did, heat from the tent blasted out, mixing with the cold.

It's so hot inside!

Panic closed Ynya's throat in a powerful grip. She was already overheating from the furs that heading inside would put her over the edge.

A quick glance around told her none of the soldiers wore any of their leathers.

There was no way Ynya was going to be able to take her

jacket off in there, and there was no way she was going to be able to keep it on with how hot she was getting.

Already Ynya's vision swam and she wasn't feeling too steady on her feet, which up till now helped sell the whole tired guardsman routine.

She'd gotten herself in over her head. She should have run, should have killed the second guard. Should never have been discovered over the body of a dead man and his mule to begin with.

Her mind wanted to spiral with worry, but she reined in her frazzled nerves.

Take it one step at a time.

She had to get to the edge of camp and take off her hat, at least for a minute or two. Then she could escape or come back or steal something. But she needed to put some distance between her and these men first.

Ynya turned, grunting something about needing to pee again.

A large form appeared in front of her. His massive chest bore battle leathers with no furs. He grabbed her by the shoulder and shoved her back a foot.

"Grof. Captain wants to see you."

Chapter Eleven

Ynya froze. The captain what? He did say Grof and not Ynya, right?

"Oi, we just got back off our shift and the Captain wants to take our man away so soon?" Her friends had noticed the order and pushed pastsheher to encircle the burly guard. "Can't a man enjoy a pint first?"

Hairs on her sweat-heavy head stood up. She didn't want a fight. But maybe if they start brawling, she could slip away.

"Yeah!" She shouted, forgetting to lower her voice.

"And she don't pay us no overtime for being out here in the cold freezing our balls off!"

"And don't forget the chores we have to do to keep this place going!"

"All we want when we get back from a long shift is to kick our feet back and spend every dime we just made on alcohol. Is that too much to ask of her majesty?"

"Alcohol!" Ynya yelled, this time her voice gruff once again. She resisted the urge to smile. This was getting fun.

"Alcohol!"

At that moment, a fierce wind blasted through the camp right into Ynya's face. The wind was so intense it filled her hood with air like a bladder. The frigid wind felt amazing on her overheated skin, dropping Ynya's body temperature by a couple degrees and pushing out most of the stuffy air from underneath her thick coats.

The others didn't fare so well, though. They'd already removed their coats and hoods before coming back out to get in the other guard's face.

All three of them were left chilled, with teeth chattering. Their faces were bright red, as if they'd been hit by frostbite.

Ynya realized it hadn't been a simple wind.

It was magic!

The guard who had come for Ynya's doppelgänger stood in the same spot, the same stern expression on his scarred and squared-off face. Along the outside of his leathers a ring of small icicles pointed toward the large tent. His face was a mix of annoyance and irritation.

The magic wind didn't come from him. The magic had to have come from behind him!

Ynya looked up with a mixture of terror and excitement. She'd never met another mage before! While, yes, her mother technically had magic, it had always been so subtly used that it was like she hadn't had it at all.

Behind the guard stood a woman dressed in a tight-fitting black leather corset and flared leather skirt split down the center. Below the skirt, she wore skin-tight pants tucked into boots. A small fur-lined hood covered her head and shoulders, and more fur cuffed her long sleeves.

Her squared-off neckline displayed her milky white skin, but a silver tattoo on her chest caught Ynya's attention, though she wasn't able to see what it was from this distance.

The woman in black was beautiful and powerful. She was everything Ynya had envisioned a mage would be.

Ynya swallowed, unsure of what to say. She couldn't stop looking at the beautiful woman.

Luckily, she didn't have to say anything, because the gruff guard wrinkled his frost covered brow. "As I said, Grof, the captain would like to speak with you."

Ynya glanced at the guard for only an instant, but by the time she looked back, the woman was gone. A ghostly imprint of her form still lingered, barely perceptible, in the falling snow.

Ynya swallowed and followed the man in silence. He led her to the larger of the tents on the edge of the camp and left her there.

"She'll come get you when she is ready. Meanwhile, I'm going show your companions what it means to earn their keep."

He turned, but not before a small, evil smile crept across his face.

A sharp shiver shot up Ynya's spine at the look. In the handful of minutes she'd gotten to know those men, she'd started to take a bit of a liking to them. They were bumbling idiots, all of them, but they had a certain charm in their camaraderie.

But then Ynya remembered why she was here and her heart grew cold.

For a moment, she had been lost in the moment, but there was no fun here, no joy. Ynya was on a mission and the last few minutes she had allowed herself to forget her goal. If those men had been party to the destruction of her home-town, then they deserved every punishment they received.

Ynya gritted her teeth and clenched her hands under the

thick coat. She needed to stay focused, she needed to keep her mind on the goal and not deviate.

Ynya glanced around, taking down her hood for a moment to clear out some of the heat. She unbuttoned her large coat and flapped it a few times to allow the biting air in and the overwhelming heat out.

She yearned to jump into the snow, to fully cool off, and soak her dress in cold, icy water, but she couldn't risk it right now.

The crunch of boots off to her side made Ynya don everything once again. This place is crawling with soldiers! They paced between the tents in a slow, methodical route, each one seemingly in time with the other, as-if a never-ending drum bore out their every step.

With her mind cooled off, Ynya could finally think.

If the woman in black is a frost mage, and I'm a fire mage, does that mean anything? Would I be more or less effective against her? I don't know! It's not like I'm able to shoot fire-balls like the wizards in the stories. All I can do is heat things up.

A wry smile crossed Ynya's lips. It was her time to do something evil. After a quick glance around for any guards, she slipped off a glove and poured heat into the tent fabric behind her.

But just as she did, the tent flap opened and the woman burst out.

"Grof! Oh, there you are, come in. I have a special project for you."

Ynya glanced down at her discarded glove. She couldn't pick it up if she wanted to, so she pulled her hand into her sleeve and followed the woman inside, grateful she'd put her hood back up already.

Ynya resumed her position inside the tent, putting both hands behind her back to mock being at attention. She had no idea if the attention was appropriate, but she used the opportunity to touch the tent fabric once again.

The woman in black grabbed a piece of parchment off her desk and shoved it at Ynya. "I have a special mission for you. I understand you're the only one of this company who can read?"

She didn't know if Grof could, but Ynya definitely could read. Her mother had taught them all from a young age.

She took the piece of parchment with her gloved hand.

A quick scan of the document told her everything she needed to know about this special mission. A quarter of the way down were four names. She flexed her jaw as she read.

Synol Oblique
    Ynya Oblique
    Finny Oblique
    Meki Oblique

ANGER FLOWED THROUGH HER IN RIVULETS. YNYA didn't even try to keep it under control, but allowed the rage to overwhelm her and ignite the tent.

Flames caught slowly and built, widening along the canvas and up toward the top. The smell of burnt cloth and rancid oil hit her nostrils.

In seconds, the entire tent was on fire.

The woman in black turned, a surprised expression on her face as she tried to comprehend how her tent had just burst into flames.

From out in the cold, someone yelled, "Fire!"

Document in hand, Ynya screamed and ran.

THE FLAMES SPREAD TO THE OTHER TENTS. THE WHOLE place had caught fire in less than a minute. The fire had been just enough chaos for Ynya to escape.

Ynya felt the magic of the mage behind her as she ran back along the road toward the dead men, the mule, and her supplies. She dumped most of the furs and dragged the dead soldier back closer to the road.

Ynya hoped it would make it look like Grof had run, even though a close examination of the body would prove otherwise. She looked at the darkening sky. She might be in luck. There was a good chance she would never been seen again with the incoming storm.

Chapter Twelve

Ynya arrived at the outskirts of Holmslatr two days later.

She re-read the parchment one more time; orders from Fellsstrond Castle asking for the capture of four known traitors to the Frost Queen. Anyone who stood in the way of their living capture would be executed according to law. It listed their names, their ages, and from where they hailed; Marsfjord.

Ynya's elation in discovery turned sour as she realized her Mama, Papa, and everyone else in the village had been murdered because the Frost Queen wanted her and her sisters.

Why?

Ynya felt sick to her stomach. Her knees buckled, unable to support her weight.

Questions swirled in her head, too many questions, but she needed to focus.

The reasons didn't matter, the methods were too long ago to debate. The most important thing was to find her sisters and get them away from the Frost Queen. Worrying about the why's and how's was a waste of time at this point.

Time continued to tick around Ynya, and every second wasted was one second her sisters traveled farther from her.

The Frost Queen.

The name seared into Ynya's mind. She'd never met anyone who had ever seen the Frost Queen, but everyone in the world knew the name. She was the ruler of the frozen north, for what that was worth, and a supposedly powerful mage. Her throne was far to the east, past Lyraville and whatever terrain lay in the Skoro district. If rumors were true, she'd been in power for over a hundred years, but Ynya knew that to be balderdash. No one lived that long.

Maybe the adults had payed attention to their supposed leader, but Ynya hadn't. It had never seemed important to her.

Maybe it would be important to her later, but right now she couldn't worry about some frost mage hundreds of miles away. She needed to find her sisters.

Finny and Meki were supposedly captured by soldiers and taken to Lyraville or beyond.

Synol was on that list too, Ynya didn't know if she was safe.

She needed to find Synol before anyone else did.

Coming up over the rise to look out on the valley below, Ynya was blown away by just how huge Holmslatr was. Stretching the entire width of the valley before her, many of the buildings had multiple stories, something she had heard was possible, but never seen with her own eyes. Trees grew from every crevice not filled with a house or other structure.

People bustled the streets here. They walked around,

chatted, and bought things from the half dozen market stalls in the center of town.

Half a dozen market stalls!

Marsfjord had one, and it was only open when you woke up cranky old man Beaunar.

Ynya stood frozen in place for minutes while she took it in. No wonder Synol had wanted to move here. She'd always been a girl too rich for simple village life. She'd never appreciated exploring caves, or hunting ice foxes in the morning.

Synol had hated the water, fishing, and small towns, and this place seemed well-suited to a girl like that.

Ynya walked into town with her head held high. She soon found herself in the market. The large road had many small shops lining each side, some looked like they had been there longer than Ynya had been alive.

She approached the first one, which seemed to be selling smoked fish. Her stomach groaned from the aroma, but Ynya didn't have any money, nor could she steal anything in broad daylight. Not now.

"Excuse me, do you know of a Synol from Marsfjord? She recently married a Torkelsen."

The shopkeep turned her head in a curious expression. "Synol from Marsfjord? Can't say I know of anyone by that name, Miss, but the Torkelsen boy, Stefan I think his name is, he did just get married, but it weren't to no lass from Marsfjord. I think she came from Kropprfjell, you know?"

Ynya thanked the woman and moved down a few more stalls.

There, a thin gentleman hammered away at some leather shoes, attaching thick soles to a set of moccasins with small metal brads.

"Hmm, sorry, young lass, you might try the ladies, they keep up with that sort of gossip better than I do."

Ynya continued her querying.

Two stalls later it was clear there was no Synol in town, and certainly no one from Marsfjord. The last woman, a candlemaker, pointed her toward the water. "My sweet Annabelle works in their house, it's just down there and left at the ship, you see?"

The massive house was at least as large as twenty from Marsfjord. It boggled her mind how these homes stand so incredibly tall!

Outside, the home had a sign from carved wood that read "Torkelsen". This had to be the place.

The only problem was a guard out front. This man didn't look like one of those bumbling idiots patrolling the road, but at least he didn't give off the sinister vibe of the women in white or black. He had to be a northerner, like her.

"Excuse me, I'm here to find my sister Synol. She came from Marsfjord and married Stefan Torkelsen."

The guard took half a step back and placed his hands on a small club attached to his belt. "Who? There is no one here by that name."

Ynya's mind slowly processed the words. After spending an hour chatting up vendors and finding the house, she wasn't ready to hear that she was still far from finding her sister.

What did it mean? Did the soldiers already gotten to Synol? Did her man already remarried after his wife's been taken from him? Was Synol just a trinket to throw away and get a new one when someone else took it from you?

The long hours spent traveling and hiding, the lack of food, and the lack of sleep caught up with Ynya. Every time she thought she was getting closer, she realized just how far away she was from any real conclusion to this mystery.

Ynya poured heat into her hand. It was time to get some answers. She'd been on the road for too long and only received more questions. She was sick of not getting anything final, of not getting closer to her goals.

Rage and frustration built under her skin. She wouldn't take no for an answer anymore.

This guard was going to tell her where her sister was.

A strong scent of sugar and alcohol hit her nostrils. A wet piece of cloth covered her mouth and nose.

Ynya looked to her side and saw an older woman smiling. She reeked of alcohol and her eyes were white and milky. Ancient burn marks around her eyes told of a long history with fire.

Ynya's head reeled. She couldn't breathe! She swam through the air and didn't know which way was up.

The woman with the scarred face told the guard. "I'm sorry, sir, my sister is a little crazy in the head. I will take her back to my home and make sure she doesn't bother you anymore."

Synol?

Then everything went black for Ynya.

Chapter Thirteen

Ynya awoke with a start. Her head pounded, but instead of a bright room and Synol sitting across from her, Ynya was surrounded by darkness.

She sat up. Pain flashed through her head as she slammed her forehead into something hard.

Ynya put her hand out and touched the thick wooden beam. She felt the dent in the corner from where her forehead crushed the fibers. The searing pain through her forehead bounced around in her skull, turning her world inside out once again.

She blacked out.

Ynya awoke with a start. Her head pounded, worse than before. A dull ache in the back and a sharp pain in the front across her forehead.

The darkness pressed in all around her. She remembered

the timber above her head and reached out of for it, placing her hand and feeling the dent once again.

Apparently, she hadn't dreamed that part.

"Synol?" She queried the darkness.

Something shuffled in the unlit room.

"Synol? Is that you?"

A small cough came from her left, then a sniffle from her right. The cough sounded like a child.

What is going on?

Ynya needed light, but she hadn't eaten in days, and her energy was running dangerously low.

Still, she needed to see, she would need to use her energy.

Grabbing a strand of hair, Ynya pinched it between her fingers and poured heat into the tips of her index finger and thumb. The heat transferred into her hair and flared to light.

It surprised her to see she was in a small room with a wooden beam roof, and a dirt floor. There was barely enough room to sit up let alone walk around.

Dozens of small dirty heads looked back at her with wide, frightened eyes.

"What is going on? Where am I?" She barked at the children. "Who are all of you?"

"I see you're awake."

A familiar voice, old and scratchy and female, came from her left.

Ynya turned. Heat coursed through her veins in time with her flaring temper.

She grabbed onto the wood above her, ready to pour heat into the structure. "I'll burn this place down if you don't let me go."

Then Ynya saw her.

The old woman seemed quite calm on the dirt floor. She held a small child in her lap and rocked gently while the kid sucked his thumb.

"You are free to go anytime you want, my dear girl. No one is holding you here other than your own clumsiness."

It was the same woman who had taken her away from the guard. She recognized the scarring around the woman's milky eyes.

Ynya suddenly felt self-conscious about her fiery threat. She dropped the heat, which she couldn't sustain much longer anyway, and lowered the light between her fingers.

"Where am I?"

"You are safe." The woman indicated the room with her free hand. "These are all refugees from the Frost Queen, hiding out from her soldiers."

Frost Queen.

Ynya tamped down the incendiary reaction to the name.

"She took my sisters."

"I know."

"How? Do you know who I am?"

The old woman smiled. She was missing four teeth, and the rest were yellowed with age, but it was still a sweet gesture. "I know you are here for Synol, but I do not know your name. In fact, half the town knows you are here for Synol. You've done a good job of that."

She licked her lips and leaned forward, pointing a wrinkled finger at Ynya. "If you want to get your sister killed, continue announcing to everyone you come across who you are and who you're looking for. Perhaps you should shout from the rooftops that you are a fire mage and you are here to find your other fire mage sister. I'm sure no one at all will tell the Skarmyord."

Ynya swallowed.

Skarmyord.

Her mother had mentioned the name late one night to her father when they thought all the girls were asleep. Ynya didn't know what it meant, but if her mother was afraid of the word, then she was too.

"My sister doesn't have magic."

The woman scoffed. "Doesn't matter if she does or not. All family members of mages are being taken to Reyoarfjell for testing."

"Testing?"

The woman nodded. "I am trying to hide as many as I can until the guards move on."

Ynya looked at the faces surrounding her. She realized now why they lived on a dirt floor with a wooden roof.

"We're under a building. This isn't a room at all, you're hiding here from the soldiers."

The woman nodded. "And I'd be much obliged if you didn't go talking about it to anyone. It's the old mill that gets used twice a week now. So we have to be silent during those times. Right now we have a little more leeway, but you still shouldn't yell. Or burn it down."

Ynya felt blood rush to her face, but not for fear or anger. She'd overreacted. This time the heat was for embarrassment.

The old woman smiled at her. Despite the scars on her face, she was a beautiful lady, with a kindly smile and mournful hollow eyes.

"You would do well to learn to keep your anger under wraps until you truly need it. The guard was about to take you in for questioning, and you don't want to do that, especially if they turn you over to the Skarmyord. You won't like the methods they use. They are so precise with their attacks and never miss. They know how to make you bleed just enough to keep you alive for as long as they need to."

Ynya didn't know what to say. She'd messed up. She had let her anger get the best of her and lash out instead of thinking things through.

Echoes of Synol's frustrations with her over the years reverberated through her head.

"Hide your intentions while readying your knife, little one. Sometimes it's better to play along then lash out. Use smoke, not fire. Smoke can be just as deadly and as painful."

Ynya nodded.

"Now, I think you were on to something with your sister. She is in there, but they don't call her by the name of Synol. They say she's not from Marsfjord, but from Kropprfjell. But I can tell you firsthand she's not from Kropprfjell."

"Why's that?"

"Because I was burned when that city was put to the torch. It's where I lost my eyes. I was a little girl back then; no one survived the stitched. That cursed place was abandoned decades ago."

Chapter Fourteen

Ynya spent the next day helping out the group of refugees under the mill.

She wouldn't abandon them after the woman had saved her from the Skarmyord.

And the woman was right. Ynya had been so focused on the anger from her mother's and father's murders that she allowed her grief to consume her thoughts. There would be a time for fire, and a time for smoke. She just needed to figure out the appropriate times and use the correct tactic.

The children were delighted to watch Ynya come back with a load of fish stolen off the boats.

They were even more delighted to see her use her magic to cook them with her bare hands.

The old woman, who the children referred to as Miss-Miss, seemed amused as well.

"That's a mighty impressive skill you have there. How old were you when you cooked your first fish like that?"

"I think I was ten. I've always been able to warm things, but as I got older I learned how to focus my energy into certain parts of my body to get the most effect. Now I can start fires if the situation is right. I learned I can light my hair the day I bloomed."

The lighted hair was something the children never got tired of, and Ynya was happy to entertain them. None of them had magic themselves. They were younger siblings or children of older mages who had been taken by the Skarmyord.

When asked about the Skarmyord, Miss-Miss refused to discuss them in front of the children. "Maybe someday, but all you need to know is that they all work for the Frost Queen, and they all have some kind of magic giving them incredible accuracy. You get one chance to kill them, because once they have a bow in their hand or a sword off their belt, they have you. If they need to keep you alive they can hobble you as easily as they would kill you. They can also take your magic from you at-will."

Ynya shuddered at the thought, and wondered if the two women she'd encountered previously had been part of the Skarmyord soldiers. There was an air about them that made her think they might have been. They hadn't been like the other soldiers.

She spent some time watching the Torkelsen house. It was obvious none of the masters were home. Half the guards napped while on duty, and the maids spent more time chatting with one another by open windows than they did changing sheets.

Miss-Miss chuckled when she learned of this. "And that's why smoke is sometimes better than fire. Imagine if you had gone in there, setting fire to the whole place just to find out no one was even home?"

That night, Ynya snuck into the market stalls and stole a

handful of simple dresses from one of the stores. She needed more for her travels, and she found a maid uniform she hoped would get her into the house easier.

She also stole blankets, sheets, and clothes for the children, ensuring they all had coverings for nighttime.

The maid uniform allowed her to walk into the manor the next morning with a load full of sheets. The same guard who had just about beaten her a couple days prior barely noticed her face, but lingered on her backside as she passed by into the house.

Ynya smiled as she kept on walking.

Men were so easy to distract.

While making herself look busy, she listened in even more on the various conversations. There was indeed a new Miss Torkelsen and the maids constantly fawned over her curly red hair.

Definitely Synol.

This new Miss Torkelsen was supposed to be some high-class lady from a far-away town.

Definitely not Synol.

This was good news, because the parchment Ynya had stolen from the guard campsite gave nothing but Synol's name and the town she came from, nothing more. Maybe Synol learned about the price on her head and changed her name? Ynya was happy to hear her sister was still alive, not captured by soldiers, and living here at this house.

Then she heard that the new Miss Torkelsen was already with child.

What?!?

Ynya dropped her load of laundry.

How is Synol already pregnant? No no no! It simply cannot be!

Can it?

When the rest of the maids moved on, she explored the massive estate. Dozens of rooms, enough to fit her entire village, made up the massive structure. Every single one had a wooden door to close it off to the rest of the home. Most of the rooms had beds and huge dressers in them, things that Ynya had only seen a few times in her village. Not one of the people she had known owned enough clothing or bedding to be able to even fill a single dresser. Old Mam owned one, though it was smaller than any of the ones she'd seen in this house.

Ynya came across a staircase. Her mother had told her about them. They allowed people to go up higher in a home. She marveled at the intricate wood carving on the railing and the plush carpet running down the middle of the wide steps. She stared for a long time, not sure if she should go up, but she was here on a mission, and she needed to keep investigating.

Be smoke, not fire.

She took the stairs one at a time, reveling at how soft the carpet was!

Ynya was at the top, where a single guard down the hallway looked at her curiously for a second, then a warm smile spread across his face.

He nodded.

She blushed.

He smiled even bigger.

She ran into the first room to the right.

Chapter Fifteen

"What were you thinking?" She leaned against the door with her back, hoping the man didn't follow her in or think she was trying to flirt with him.

"You have got to keep your emotions in check, Ynya." She said again, hoping he couldn't hear anything out there.

She listened, but didn't hear any footsteps. Her mind caught up with her emotions. There was a guard inside the house.

Why would there ever been a guard inside a house for a specific room? There wouldn't be...unless there was something in there to protect.

She needed to test her theory.

After few minutes of clanking around in the room she was in, Ynya peeked her head out of the door and stared down the hallway. Sure enough, the same house soldier stood in loose attention in front of the same door.

He was young, probably about her age, with hints of stubble dusting his squared jaw. His brown eyes matched his unruly hair. He was attractive. Probably the first man Ynya had ever looked at and thought this way about.

Gathering up her linens, she walked down the hallway, making eye contact with him once more. She let a slight smile grace her lips.

Not too flirty.

She slowed as she approached the door, testing to see if the man would step out of the way.

He smiled back and nodded, but didn't move. In fact, it almost looked like he dug in his heels and tensed his body.

He's definitely guarding the door.

It was time for another plan. She kept going like she'd planned to, stopping outside the next door with her hand on the ornate knob that probably cost more than her entire house.

Ynya put on her happiest face and smiled back at him. She'd never been courted, so she wasn't entirely sure how to make faces at men. She hoped this would work.

Their eyes met once again and she held the pose for a few seconds, making sure her eye contact lingered for long enough. Finally, she nodded in the direction of the door, then turned the knob and entered.

As soon as she did so, a woman screamed, followed by a man's deep bellowing voice.

Ynya took in the sight before her. It was all pale skin and bed linens. Black hair and nakedness.

"I'MSOSORRYIDIDN'TMEANTOCOMINHERE!"

She slammed the door so fast that she didn't get her foot away in time and stubbed her big toe on the thick wooden slab.

Ynya stood there for a moment, her hand hovering just over the doorknob as she tried to calm herself. The guard down the hall snickered as the couple inside the room began to argue.

Heat flooded her face. She didn't know if it was embarrassment or anger. Probably a little of both.

Ynya turned, reacting to the heat rising in her body and walked past the guard toward the other room.

As she walked, she grabbed the man's hand with her own, a bolt of exhilaration shooting through her arm as she did so, but she ignored the sensation. She was on a mission.

The man barely seemed to resist as Ynya pulled him into the empty room on the other side of the house. She practically threw him toward the bed and shut the door behind her.

He stood there all smiles and nervousness. He opened his mouth to say something and just stood there, mouth agape.

With a couple running steps, she jumped into his arms, knocking him onto the bed and poured heat into his head.

In seconds, he had overheated and was knocked out.

"That'll teach you for laughing at my misfortune."

Ynya opened the door to the guarded room. Her town had one room like this, with a chair and a desk, and other furniture scattered around holding various books and papers.

It was a bit warm in this room, however. It was a good thing she was just here to snoop and explore, because all the excess heat she'd expended on the guard plus this toasty room made her feel a little woozy.

She wasn't worried, though. Ynya just needed a few minutes to explore the room and she would go back outside to cool off.

It was a beautiful room, with dark stained woods and soft velvet fabrics covering the windows. It was masculine, and pain for her Papa shot through her heart for a moment until she shoved it back down with the rest of her emotions.

The desk contained a number of books and papers. She opened up the topmost book to yellowed pages containing hundreds of crisscrossing lines forming squares on the page. Numbers and words were written in those. It had to be a ledger. She'd seen a book like this at the one shop in Marsfjord.

She lifted up the book, which ended up being a lot heavier than she thought, and looked at the large paper beneath. This one wasn't as yellow as the pages in the book, but the calligraphy and design work on the page were impressively ornate.

It's a marriage certificate!

Ynya's heart beat faster as she scanned down through the document.

The two names listed were Stefan Torkelsen and Sarah Oblit.

"Sarah Oblit?"

It was close enough to Synol Oblique that it had to be her sister.

Ynya's heart raced faster once again as she read through the rest of the document. It listed where and when they married, and a couple witnesses, but nothing else.

She flipped over the license to take in another document.

Her heart skipped a beat when she saw the dragon skull insignia in the upper right corner. She'd seen that before, but she couldn't quite remember where.

Ynya turned the large page over to find blood-red wax fragments. It was a broken seal from the letter.

She folded up the page and the same bony dragon skull was etched in the top right corner of the page.

Ynya glanced at the door, wondering how much longer she had until the guard awoke. She needed to hurry.

Her heart racing once again, she reopened the page and started reading.

This one looked like a bill of sale, but she wasn't sure what it meant.

No names were on the page, but it stipulated an exchange of sorts was being made. It referred to another document stating that if the location of the target was found and handed over, then the owner of this document was free to do what they wanted with their property, provided proper testing ensure the property was of no use to Her Majesty.

Her Majesty.

The Frost Queen wanted something and had sent them a document giving them something else in exchange for it.

What is this document referring to?

Ynya re-read the whole document again, looking for more clues, then folded it up and stuffed it into her pocket. Maybe Miss-Miss knew something about it.

She then opened up the top drawer of the desk to look for anything else that gave her more information on where her sister might be at this moment.

Ynya hoped she wouldn't find anything else marked with the sinister skull.

Chapter Sixteen

Ynya continued to root through the drawers but found nothing of interest. All she could find were more ledgers and documents detailed the holdings of the family's boats and houses.

She found a nice dagger in there as well, ornate carvings and silver blade. She took it, of course.

Noises sounded in the hallway.

Ynya paused. It sounded like a man and woman's voice. Possibly the couple from next door?

Ynya found her face flushing once again at the memory. That was an image she would never get out of her head. Who knew a man's backside was so hairy?

She continued to the next drawer when the office door burst open.

Ynya jumped. It was the guard she knocked out!

He pointed at her and yelled, but his eyes were doing something strange as they wobbled around in his sockets.

Oh uh, I hope I didn't cook his brain too much.

"Her!"

She smiled. "Yes, it was me, but you see you were–"

Then the door behind him filled with soldiers.

Uh oh.

He'd already gone for reinforcements, and she'd been so engrossed with her search that she hadn't payed attention to noises outside of the room.

Ynya whirled around, looking for any way of egress, but there was only one door. She ran behind the desk to the large window behind it, but didn't see any way of opening it.

What kind of useless window doesn't open to let in fresh air?

The previous build-up of heat combined with the stale air in the room hit her. She stumbled. Ynya'd forgotten that she had been overheating by the time she came into this room.

Ynya looked up to assess the threat between her and freedom.

Three guards came at her. Two fresh ones plus the bloke she'd knocked out on the bed. He still wobbled where he stood, and since he was the one guarding the door, taking him out would allow Ynya's escape the easiest.

She grabbed a book off the desk and threw it at the man to her left. She dove to the right and tackled the second man, preparing her magic to lash at him. However her hands landed on a thick leather chest piece protecting his chest.

Ynya worked her hands up to his head to try to overheat him as well, but he kneed her in her stomach, sending her reeling onto the floor.

Her stomach spasmed from the blow and her lungs burned along with her stomach.

Her mouth worked like a fish out of water with no way to pull in air.

Ynya rolled again as the man got to his feet and balled up his fists.

She focused, trying to take in her surroundings once again. Ynya had one shot to get out of this.

The first guard came at her from over the desk. The second guard was on his feet in a low crouch about to punch her in the gut again. Bed guard loomed over her, seeming unable to formulate a plan. He stood on shaky legs above her head, still trying to focus on the fight.

Taking him out was still the better plan.

Ynya rolled backwards and kicked as hard as she could right in between his legs. The full force of her attack sent him flying with a high-pitched squeak into guard number two.

She rolled backwards, still unable to breathe. Her lungs burned, but she refused to stop running. She had to get out.

Ynya paused in the doorway, taking in the hallway to make a fast decision.

A man stood on the stairs along with two maids.

Are they enlisting the help of the staff to catch me?

Ynya remembered a window, among other things, when she glanced into the room with the two lovers. Best of all, she remembered it was open.

Yes!

Turning right, she sprinted as her heart hammered in her chest with each shaky footstep.

She was overheating, and she struggled to pull in breath still. As Ynya ran down the hallway her vision swam around her, but she focused on the door as her vision grew black.

Just have to make it outside.

She rounded the door, grateful it was open, and saw water.

All she had to do was make it out of the window and into the ocean and she would be back to new.

Behind her, a scuffle of boots and grunts reminded her that the men weren't that far behind. Ynya tried to count them but there were too many.

Why am I counting, anyway? What do I hope to accomplish by counting feet?

It's because feet mattered, and she knew that for a fact.

As she flew through the doorway, Ynya slapped the wooden door to close it behind her, but it hit something hard and bounced back, knocking her foot to the side just enough that it tripped up her gate.

See? I told you feet mattered.

Ynya stumbled into the bed and rolled. Her wild hands grabbed at anything she could hold, which was slightly sweaty bedding.

Wow, you are very sweaty! Ynya, the very sweaty girl. Now go wash up before dinner!

She hit the headboard with a solid thunk, finally able to draw in a partial breath to her burning lungs.

The room wavered and swam before her. She probably looked like that poor guard she'd just kicked.

Poor man with so many booboos!

What is wrong with me?

Her head wasn't thinking straight.

Somewhere, deep in the recesses of her mind, she was aware that she had overheated, and the lack of air to her body was making her go slowly insane.

Yes, all the booboos!

Ynya tried to get up, but she was trapped. She felt something soft around her, but couldn't quite figure out what it was.

"Haul her down to interrogation before the family gets back."

Shadows loomed over her. Ynya tried to kick but each movement was like swimming through a vast, hot ocean.

One of the shapes spoke, but she didn't know if it speaking to her or the others.

It was so pretty, like an angel above her.

Ynya tried to reach out to touch the angel but her hand wouldn't move.

Everything was all right though, because she slipped deeper into the shadow as the angels moved above her.

Chapter Seventeen

Ynya slept for a long time, while visions of black birds, dragons, and her mother swam in her head.

She remembered being moved. Was it by the angels? No, it was the guards. She knew that now. She'd overheated and hallucinated some things. It was all too much for her. Her body had done what it needed to keep her alive.

No time.

"I'm sorry, Mama. I'm sorry I keep making mistakes."

Time, Ynya. No time.

"I'm sorry I haven't found Synol yet. I'm sorry I refused to see her get married."

"Who's Synol?"

Ynya wasn't talking to her mother, nor was she talking to her angels. She was talking to one of the guards.

It was the book guard, the first one. Behind him was gut punch guard.

She didn't see the other one. She did feel bad about what she'd done to him.

Still deserved it.

"Are you talking about Mrs. Torkelsen?"

She shook her head. "Water."

"Not till you answer my questions."

"Water." It was a struggle to say anything at all, with how dehydrated she was.

Her eyes burned, despite the room barely having any light at all. She was soaked through with sweat from being wrapped in the blankets.

Ynya still felt the lingering effects of the punch to her stomach, and the overheating.

She was severely dehydrated. Her body must have done all it could to shed heat, and barring her breath, which she realized now just how important breathing hard was to maintain her elevated body temperature, she'd sweat profusely.

It also explained why she'd gotten so delirious there at the end.

Ynya was tied to a chair. The bonds cut into her skin, probably the men's anger from having to work extra hard that day. It was fine. She probably deserved it for kicking and punching them, but she needed to get out of here. She needed to escape.

"Water, then talk." She managed to squeak out.

The guard growled. "Get her some water."

The other guard grabbed a skin from a dark corner and shoved it in her mouth.

Ynya guzzled water, draining the entire skin, or at least the amount that didn't pour down her chest.

I'm like a dog. Guzzling water that splashes everywhere and panting to stay cool.

She licked her lips to get every last drop into her mouth. "Get me more, but we can start talking now."

Ynya needed more to properly cool off and get enough energy to break her bonds.

The first guard grabbed another chair, flipped it backwards and sat down, his legs splayed out behind the back.

Maybe he did that to protect himself after what she did to the last guard.

She smiled.

"Think you're so funny, huh? Sneaking in here looking like a maid. What were you here to steal, huh?"

The fire raged within her once again. "I'm not here to steal anything, you witless oaf. Did I take anything? What about all those jewels displayed in the bedroom? Did I take any of those? Or did you notice the others using the bedroom for other things?"

She was spitting at the man by the end of her tirade.

Calm down, Ynya. Smoke, not fire.

Ynya took a long breath, closing her eyes in the process. She needed to relax. Using up valuable energy on this moron wasn't going to help anything.

Smoke.

"I'm here looking for my sister."

The guards glanced at each other. "Your sister? Is she a maid here?"

Once again, the stupid questions itched at the back of her head, begging to get unleashed back at him, but she shoved them back down.

Smoke, not fire.

She couldn't help it. She was tired of dealing with idiots and snapped at the man.

"Do you see my hair? Do you see what color it is? Is there anyone else in this household that looks like me? Maybe a couple years older than me? Maybe she just showed up to this house a couple months ago? Got married? Is any of this making it through your thick skull?"

All right, maybe just a little fire.

The man got a stricken expression on his face and whirled around to glance at his partner, who stood in the shadow, frowning.

"How do we know you're not lying. Hair can be dyed. Or maybe you're a siren from the depths here to lure us away. You did try to seduce Jan after all."

After another long, calming breath, Ynya addressed the guard in the back. She dug through her memories to remember all the details she'd seen on the marriage certificate, plus the rumors of the recent marriage she'd heard from the shopkeepers.

"My name is Ynya Oblit. I hail from Kropprfjell to the southeast. My sister married your master, Stefan Torkelsen. At the time of the marriage, which was two months ago on the full moon, I was unable to make it here, but I travelled all this way to see my sister. She told me to just come in and the staff would treat me like royalty. I can see clearly that you do not, in fact, treat anyone with the station they have, but rather accuse us of misdeeds and tie us up like common criminals!"

A different kind of fire burned just behind her eyes this time. It was a cool fire, something she felt when she lied to her sisters about how safe the jump was going to be, or trying to convince Synol not to tell Mama about her latest antics.

It wasn't a fire she was able to control, but it came in handy, and she was glad it reared its head this time.

"Go ahead, check my story. Shopkeepers will remember I came into town a couple days ago asking about my sister.

Check my hair against any she left behind on a hairbrush. You will see they match."

The two guards stared at one another for a moment, seemingly trying to come up with a solution to this mess. The one in the shadow cocked his head to one side, motioning the other guard to get up.

They left the room.

"Hey! Don't forget I need more water!"

Chapter Eighteen

✦❀✦

They left her alone for a while.

Unfortunately, without more food or water, Ynya didn't have enough energy to burn through the ropes.

Even if she did, she worried would catch the rug she sat on or set the wooden chair on fire.

And that would just burn down Synol's new home.

The place crawled with staff at the moment. Dozens of voices shouted in the distance. Doors opened and closed. The clomp of boots ran up and down the hallway. Something was clearly going on outside her little room.

Even if she escaped, Ynya might be able to take out a maid or two, but any guards with even the remotest amount of training would just capture her again. And she didn't think they would restrain their angry blows this time.

The best thing for her to do was wait, bide her time, and hope they brought her enough food to regain her energy.

With enough energy, anything was possible.

The door slammed open, and the two guards filled the doorway.

"Did you bring water?"

The one in the back scoffed. "You had enough water."

Worry crept up her spine but she ignored it. Ynya would figure out something. The staff had to leave at some point, go home their own lives, and once it was down to just her and one or two other guards, then she could always burn the whole house down and use the fire to escape.

"Fine. If that is how you are going to play it, then my sister will be hearing about the way you have treated me, and you, both of you, won't have your jobs in the morning. Enjoy them while you can."

"Oh, don't you worry about Miss. We've contacted the Queen's royal soldiers. They were quite interested in meeting you. They are sending over their top interrogators to personally escort you to Reyoarfjell."

Ynya's blood froze right in her veins at the mention of the location.

She swallowed. "You mean the Skarmyord?"

The guard got a big grin on his face. "I see you know about them. They are going to love you."

Ynya willed her fear back down.

Her heat rose once again, burning off precious energy. Energy she might need to burn down this house soon.

One of the guards kneeled down before her, sticking his face close to hers.

"They're giving out nice rewards to anyone who turns over someone like you. We don't need to have these jobs anymore with as much as they will give us to hand you over to them."

Her mind raced, but she tried to keep a level head and a serene face on the outside.

The other guard picked a knife up from his scabbard and

tossed it into the air, catching it with his gloved hand. "Since you know about the Skarmyord, you know how deadly they are, right?"

"Oh yeah," the kneeling guard replied, "they're legendary around here. Trained from birth."

"Imbued with magic."

"Helps guide all their attacks."

"They don't miss. Even inches from death, in massive pain, they never miss."

"Oh, and don't get us started on how they get information from people."

"You will tell them everything."

"Everything."

"They know how to hurt you in such a way that you will never die, but the pain will be so intense that you will wish you were dead."

"Imagine how bad it's going to be."

"Stop!" Ynya screamed, her mind racing faster than she could process. "Stop talking, alright? You got your point across!"

The first guard stood up, a wry smile on his face. "I think she understands, don't you?"

"Oh yeah."

"But first, we have a little payback in store for you, in honor of our buddy Jan. He told us to make you sing all high pitched like he is now."

The guard balled up his fist and punched her in the gut.

The pain lanced through her stomach, knocking the wind out of her once again.

"No! Please!" Ynya tried to talk, but the words came out as breathless whispers.

"Sorry, I didn't hear that, you're going to have to speak up if you want us to listen to you."

He reared back and punched her in the jaw, knocking her head backward with a snap.

The door burst open, startling the guards.

Ynya tried to open her eyes but they were filled with tears, unable to see. Her ears rung from the blow, but the voice from the doorway was unmistakable.

"Get away from my sister!"

A lithe form with red hair rushed through the room and stopped in front of Ynya. "What have they done to you?"

Synol whirled around at the stunned guards. "I said leave her alone! Get out of here and never come back! You are both fired and if you do not leave this house this instant I will have you both arrested for assaulting a maiden."

The guards hesitated for a second, looking at each other, then they looked to the door where a man stood. He was a few years older than Ynya, with long black hair pulled to a ponytail. He wore the fanciest clothes she'd ever see on a man, almost like a dress for a lady. He nodded to the guards.

"You heard my wife. You are done here. Get out of here before I remember your names."

Both guards rushed from the room.

Synol turned back to Ynya, cupping her face in her hands.

Heat from the blow still pulsed in Ynya's face, but her sisters' hands felt so cool on her burning skin.

"Hoy, Syni. Can I get some water?"

Chapter Nineteen

✦✦✦

"Can we get her some food and water?"

Synol undid Ynya's ties, allowing the ropes to drop to the floor.

"Of course, my love."

Stefan leaned out of the doorway to bark orders at the staff.

"Are you hurt?" Synol's voice sounded much like Mama's as she looked over Ynya's body for injury.

Ynya smiled. "Nothing worse than I've gotten in the past. Remember when I fell down that crevasse?"

Synol drew her lips to a line and her eyes went wide with alarm.

Her eyes bored into Ynya's for a fierce second before relaxing. "My husband will be bringing food and water. For now we need to get you cleaned up."

Ynya thought she knew what Synol was so worried about. Can't let anyone know you have magic. It was the same thing Ynya had to do all growing up whenever someone not from the town was around.

Like it was some family secret or something.

A shudder went down Ynya's spine at the thought. It was a secret, and it leaking might have gotten her family killed.

The weight of her quest slammed into her, and whatever smart retort Ynya was about to say disappeared into the black haze as she realized just what her Mama had meant all these years.

She'd been too young to understand. It was critical that she keep her magic hidden. Now it was quite clear. Now it was too late.

It was too late for anyone now. The secret was out and her family was dead.

It was all her fault.

Ynya burst into tears and slumped onto Synol's shoulder.

Just like her Mama before her, Synol took Ynya in her arms and rubbed her back.

"I'm here now, Ynya. I'm here."

They stayed locked like that for a long time. Each in her sister's arms like they should be. All the fighting and bickering from the past and they were here for each other now.

The food arrived, and Synol broke. She stood and smoothed down her dress. The prim and proper Synol was back. Ynya needed the other Synol.

"Synol, we need to talk. It's about Mama and Papa."

"Get this girl some food." Stefan pointed to the floor in front of Ynya.

Ynya locked eyes with her sister, pleading with her to get rid of the extra people so the two could talk. Food could wait.

"Come, eat." Stefan picked up a pickled egg and tried to hand it to her.

"I need to talk to my sister. Something has happened."

Stefan's expression changed in a heartbeat. He dropped

the egg back to the platter and stood, taking Synol in his arms with his hands around her midsection.

Slowly, his hands worked their way around her hips, dipping low on her abdomen before resting under her stomach.

Synol tensed at the motion, like she wasn't entirely comfortable that a man had his hands placed this low on her body.

Ynya felt the heat rising once again in her head. She didn't care if she was smoke or fire anymore.

"I'm afraid that any discussion around Sarah will need to remain...clean, shall we say. As you can probably tell from the glow she now has, she is with child and we must think of the health of the baby above all else." His voice had an edge to it that Ynya had heard many times from her mother when it was clear she didn't want to talk about something.

Ynya remembered the staff talking about Synol's pregnancy earlier, but her sister barely looked pregnant at all, her stomach just barely sticking out. She must not be very far along.

He craned his neck over to kiss her on the cheek. The action seemed to calm Synol a bit. Her face muscles relaxed and she returned a small smile. She even placed one of her hands over one of his.

Watching the two hold each other like that made a shiver travel up Ynya's spine.

"Besides, Sarah's family is perfectly safe back in Kropprf-jell, aren't they, my love?"

Synol nodded, a mechanical, hollow motion meant to convey exactly what she was required to, and nothing more.

Ynya finally understood why Synol was going by Sarah. She was hiding in plain sight.

The red hair was unheard of this far north, and with the recent decree by the Frost Queen, they probably decided to use this marriage as a way for her to change her name and place of birth in order to hide her true identity.

The marriage to this wealthy merchant family suddenly made more sense to Ynya. What better family to hide you than one with the resources to whisk you away to safety should the Frost Queen come around looking?

But none of that mattered now. Ynya made a promise to her mother and she was going to do everything she could to get Synol out of here.

Ynya snorted. "No matter, I just needed to eat anyway."

Both Stefan and Synol relaxed.

Synol waved behind her at a servant who brought her a chair. After sitting down across from Ynya, she gave a strained smile. "Yes. Let us eat together. Just like old times."

Ynya ate, but the whole time, her mind churned.

Had Mama planned this marriage the whole time? Had she been working on a place for me to go as well? Did she tell Synol about this plan?

Or was there a plan at all? Maybe this was all just coincidence. Maybe none of the plan was from Mama.

The void across the table terrified Ynya, and Synol attempted to fill it with idle chatter.

"Stefan has found me the finest doctor who says the baby is quite healthy. They can already tell, you know."

"Mmm." Ynya replied, still lost in thought.

"Yes, and how was your trip in from Kropprfjell? How are things back there to the south? I should like to visit someday, but not until the baby is old enough to travel of course." She glanced over at her husband who gave a small nod.

"Of course, my lovely bride is going make the most wonderful mother, don't you think, Ynya?"

Ynya looked up at the question. *How dare he mention mothers around me.*

The rage under her skin yearned to slap the man. She needed to talk to her sister, and it had to be alone. None of this mindless discussion was going to do anything useful.

"I do think Synol," both of them flinched at the use of her real name, "will make a wonderful mother, but I have some news about our own mother, you know. There is a reason I came here."

Chapter Twenty

"Hmm," Stefan halfheartedly mumbled as he reached for a hunk of cheese. "I should love to hear about it tonight at dinner. My own father will of course be celebrating the arrival of my bride's sister and the small babe."

Ynya took another bite from her roll, chewing faster than she should. She felt her blood begin to boil at Stephan's overprotective nature.

Every little thing he did irritated her now. The way he smiled with only the corners of his mouth. The way he sipped from his cup twice instead of once. The creepy way he glanced at her sister.

Ynya understood him wanting to keep bad news from Synol at this time, but this game they played was beyond frustrating. She just needed to talk to her sister.

She'd heard the stories of how the wealthy danced around topics instead of addressing them head-on, and there was a reason she didn't like them.

If Synol wanted to marry into a family who played those

games, fine, it's her life, but Ynya's patience wore thin. She needed to try a new tactic.

"Actually, Stefan, I need to talk to my sister about some... womanly issues."

Stefan halted his chewing mid bite. Crumbs from his cracker fell back out of his mouth.

"Womanly?" He replied with his mouth full of dry cracker.

Ynya smiled. "Yes, you see I have recently come of age and I need to discuss with my older sister about my mooncycle."

Stefan coughed, spraying un-chewed cracker across the bowl of fruit in front of him.

"Oh," he said, still unable to swallow the dry concoction still coating the insides of his mouth, "I should let you two get on with it."

About time.

She returned her most polite smile as he got up.

Stefan's chair scraped across the floor and almost toppled, but he caught it at the last second. Moments later, he was out the door and into the hallway.

"When are you going to grow up?" Synol finally interjected. She nodded backwards at the closed door. "Did you have to bring that up in front of him?"

Ynya's irritation slipped right into that comfortable groove she'd been building up for years with Synol.

"How else was I supposed to get him out of here? Are you on such a short leash that you cannot be with your own sister for even a few minutes without him being here to chaperone you?"

Synol looked like she was going to snap back at her sister,

but instead leaned back in her chair and put her hand back to her stomach. "Things have changed, Ynya, and I have bigger things to think about than catching up with my favorite sister."

Ynya refused to be baited with the favorite part. "Yes, Synol Oblique, things sure have changed and now I have to wonder if you knew about them all along because of how casual you are being right now. You are right. There are bigger things to think about."

Ynya's vision was red now, with plenty of energy to fuel her righteous indignation.

"The reason I came here was to tell you that Finny and Meki have been ca–"

The door swung open and Stefan's form filled the room. "Oh good, things are civil here, but just in case my dear wife needs any assistance, for the baby of course, I have brought her wet-nurse and handmaid, Edith and Lena. I've also summoned the doctor to be on standby just in case."

Synol tilted her head back and nodded to her husband. "Thank you, my dear. You are always looking out for all the little details when my mind is not all here."

Stefan smiled at his wife, then his eyes flickered over to Ynya for a second before turning from the door.

She could swear that his eyes held nothing but malice for her. Ynya had already stopped mid-sentence when Stefan entered the room again, but she lost all train of thought at those eyes.

Why is he mad at me? Shouldn't he be happy to see his sister-in-law visiting his wife? What is going on?

"You were saying?" Synol grabbed her cup of water and took a sip.

Ynya glanced to the two terrified nurses standing in the corner. "I..." One was small and petite, while the other was round with a fussy look about her. Both women looked mortified to be in here and Ynya wondered what made them look like they did. Surely, talk of mooncycles shouldn't bother them.

Synol filled in the vacancy of conversation. "Forgotten already? Now were you here to discuss womanly issues or was that just another excuse to get me into trouble?"

"Me, get you into trouble? I told you dozens of times to just let me go, but you had to stay with me. You just couldn't let me get in trouble on my own, because you were always looking out for me. Well it's not my fault you stuck around, it was your decision, not mine."

"Is that what you think? You think I wanted to get in trouble with Mama? I did it because I was trying to take care of my little sister who refused to go a full day without sticking her nose somewhere it didn't belong."

In the back of her mind, a small voice tried to remind Ynya of why she was here. She heard it, but she chose to ignore it for the more pressing insult before her. Sometimes, despite all logic telling you not to engage, the correct answer was the one right in front of you, and she had plenty to deal with from that last comment.

"Well, of course as soon as I need someone in my life, you up and get married to some rich guy to the south. It's like you couldn't wait to get away from us. It's like you just wanted to get away from your family."

Synol steeled her eyes and quickly glanced at her nurses before back at Ynya. "My family? I have a family, Ynya. I started it when I married my husband, and my love for him does not change my feelings for Mama, Papa, or anyone else."

She sat back in her chair, tossing her head to the side so Ynya could see her mouth the final words.

"Including you."

Chapter Twenty-One

꧁꧂

Y nya couldn't speak. Her mouth refused to move, and her brain stopped working.

All the rage and anger building up under her skin faded in a flash of heat through her eyes.

Of course Synol had to say that. She always talked everything around a topic, without addressing it directly. It should infuriate Ynya, but this time it didn't.

Synol was right, and she had gotten under Ynya's skin.

No, that's not right.

Ynya had allowed Synol to get under her skin. Ynya had showed up unannounced to her new home, broken in and injured the staff. She had worried her pregnant sister and her new husband.

Then, when my sister and her overprotective husband find out about me, they me some food and water, they make small talk while the staff works in the background to try to reset the house to how it was, and I start mouthing off to my pregnant sister while also forgetting about the whole reason I'd had come here in the first place.

How could I be so stupid?

Smoke, not fire.

Ynya was the one causing problems, and she was the one making it about herself.

Her sisters were the only thing that mattered now.

"Sarah," she used the name she knew the staff would recognize. "I'm sorry. I didn't mean to come here to talk about old wounds, I came to talk about new ones."

This got the attention of the two women, who both took a step forward from the corner.

The larger of the two stuck her hand out to interrupt. "I'm afraid Miss–"

Ynya stood, pointing a dangerous finger at the two. "This is too important not to tell, now sit down or I will sit you down."

They both sat, but remained on the edges of their seats.

Ynya turned to her sister, who had a curious but concerned look on her face.

"Synol, you need to listen to me. Mama and Papa are dead. Men came to the village and burned it the ground. Finny and Meki were taken and I need your help to get them back."

Synol kept her expression blank as she listened, then replied with a cautious smile. "Are you insane? You come all the way down here to play some silly game with me? Have you not caused enough grief in my life?" She turned to the staff in the corner. "I think I should like to go now, it's getting a bit too stuffy in this room, and my sister will be heading home now."

The women stood.

Ynya leapt across the table, standing in front of the doorway.

"No one is leaving this room until you listen to me, Synol. Listen!"

She pulled the burned necklace from under her shirt and thrust it at her sister. "Do you see? That's Mama's blood, Synol. Her blood is on this necklace from when she was stabbed in the chest."

She opened her palm, showing off the ring. "Papa's ring, from where he died trying to get to Mama, with his axe in his back."

Synol looked between the two, a mortified expression on her face.

"Ynya, what are you–"

"They are both *dead*, Synol. That is why I came here to tell you."

The women in the corner screamed, calling for help.

Ynya glared at them but it was too late now. She had to finish telling her tale. This might be her only chance.

"Mama was raped while Papa bled out, unable to move. I put down her dress myself. She held on for two days waiting for me to come home, Synol. Two days!"

Ynya grabbed Synol's hands, wrapping them around the necklace.

"She held on after being stabbed and raped, and laid there in the snow the whole time waiting for one of her daughters to come home. She suffered the ultimate indignity just to see me one last time and you know what she asked me to do? Come find you! Her only thoughts were about her daughters and making sure they were safe."

Ynya took a pleading step toward her sister.

Synol's entire body trembled.

"Synol," Ynya lowered her voice almost to a whisper. "She gave it to me, Synol. Her gift. I don't know what it is yet, but she put her hands on my head and she passed me—"

The door burst open, slamming into Ynya's side. The surprise entrance knocked her from her sister's grasp.

But in the doorway was not Stefan, it was the woman in black from the last encampment.

She smiled at Ynya.

Ynya grabbed for the ever-burning flame inside her, but the woman in black was too fast. In a brilliant flash of steel, the woman stabbed Ynya three times; once in her left thigh, one one her right stomach, and once in her left shoulder.

Three fast jabs and Ynya dropped to the floor.

She couldn't move.

What is this sorcery? Her whole body was numb, like when she had slept on her arm. Her magic receded from her grasp as well, still there, but out of reach.

The woman smiled again and pulled Ynya up onto a chair.

"I'm glad we had a chance to meet once again, Ynya *Oblique*. I've been looking for you for a while now. I was almost beginning to wonder where you had gone."

She whirled around, her skirt leathers slapping Ynya in the face. "Take her."

Ynya still couldn't move, couldn't talk, and couldn't do anything with her magic.

Synol cried to the side. "Please let her go! She didn't know what she was doing!"

Stefan showed up and guided his wife out of the room.

On her way out, the woman produced a small pouch of jingling coins. She stopped in front of a man that looked like an older version of Stefan Torkelsen, and dropped the pouch in his outstretched hand. He bowed to her, but she continued to walk down the hallway like she owned the home. Steady, casual, and sure of herself.

Watching the woman walk confidently down the hallway was the impetus Ynya needed to put all the pieces of the puzzle together. She knew what she had been missing this whole time.

The letters calling for all four of the sister's capture, the fake names on the marriage certificate, the sealed letter from the Frost Queen.

It all made sense. The letter wasn't to Stefan, it was to the father. The father who owned this house and used the fancy office upstairs.

He'd made a pact with the Frost Queen for his son to marry Synol.

He was the one who betrayed their location.

He was the one who killed her family.

He was the one who had to die.

Chapter Twenty-Two

Soldiers came and dragged Ynya away. She didn't see Synol or her husband at all, but she did lock eyes with the man of the house, the one carrying the new coin purse.

He was a shrewd man, dangerously thin, and his long pointed nose looked like it had been broken a few times. His angular face had a permanent scowl on it. Even when smiling he looked like a jester all dressed up to look sad.

Ynya memorized every line on his face, every mole, every crease. She would not forget his face.

She would burn that face.

Part of Ynya felt bad for the way she told her sister about their parents. She wondered if Synol believed her or if she would have taken the hint. Ynya hadn't wanted it to happen like it did, but it was the only way she was able to get the information out. Now she wondered if she should have just blurted it out right when she saw her sister and dealt with the ramifications afterward.

At least then she would have been able to escape before the guards showed up.

After marching her across town, the soldiers threw Ynya into a cell at the city prison.

The iron bars clanged shut. She could only lie there, paralyzed. She heard noises in the room, hushed whispers and scuffs. Humans. At least she wasn't alone, and the stone floor had some straw on it to cushion her fall.

It took fifteen long minutes until Ynya could move again, but strangely, her powers still didn't come back. She felt them just in the background, but was unable to pull them forth.

Maybe I'm cursed. Maybe this is going to be my life for now.

She fought to keep the dark thoughts from swirling around her, but all her mistakes swam through her mind like a bad dream.

The worst part was that she was cold. Her blocked magic wasn't able to keep her body heat up and the cool floor sapped her heat even more. Even swimming in the ocean surrounded by hunks of ice, she'd never felt this cold before!

Ynya turned around, taking in the figures in the dark room.

An older man with a thick beard and earrings stood from the bench. "Are you all right Miss?"

Ynya nodded, stretching her sore arms. "Where are we?"

"Jail, of course," a girl from the bench stated. She didn't bother looking at Ynya, but stared at the ceiling.

"What are they going to do with us?"

The man extended a hand, which Ynya took. "I'm Firtz, nice to meet you."

"Ynya."

Firtz continued. "The Frost Queen mandates all mages

are to be taken to Reyoarfjell for testing. Any found valuable are pressed into service."

He spat on the ground to punctuate his point.

Ynya wanted to do the same, but she hadn't eaten or drunk enough at her sister's house to be able to afford the moisture.

Her magic stirred, a small portion of it coming forth. She felt the familiar heat just under her skin once again. For a while there, she was beginning to get terribly cold, something she'd rarely experienced before in her life.

"Does anyone know what they are testing for?"

Firtz's eyes hardened. "No one truly knows. The only thing for sure is that once you go to Reyoarfjell, you never go back home."

"Fantastic."

Ynya walked up to the bars, her limbs still stiff from the strange attack with the silver blade. She pulled her dress to the side to look at the wound in her shoulder. A small black mark remained where she'd been punctured, but no blood had seeped out.

Odd.

Her magic was coming back, though in a diminished capacity. Her skin warmed up to bring her now-cool body back up to where she was comfortable.

"What is that weapon they use? The silver dagger."

The girl spoke up again. "I don't think they have a name, but they stop you from being able to access your own magic. It's their best way to control you. Depending on how they hit you, they can turn off your speech, your magic, and your ability to move."

Ynya snickered, grabbing the cold rusty bars. "Seems I was a triple threat because I got all three."

"We're sorry for leaving you on the ground. Touching anyone who has been stabbed can be incredibly painful for us. Only non-mages are able to handle someone who has been hit by those blades."

Ynya nodded. "It's understandable. So, what are we going to do to get out of here?"

Silence.

She turned, meeting each set of eyes. She saw it then, the lack of fight in any of them.

"Six mages in a room and none of us can come up with a way to get out of here? There is only one of them out there, right? The woman with the black leather dress?"

Three of them shook their heads while two more turned away.

"There is the woman in white."

"And the man in red."

"And the twins."

"The twins?" Ynya asked.

Everyone grew silent.

"All right, so no one wants to talk about the twins, but we still can get out of here, can't we?"

The girl stood. "If you try to use your magic in here, it will alert the Skarmyord and they will punish you for it. It's... it's not pleasant. Worse than what you just went through." She looked down at her feet, a solemn look on her face. "I'm Joanne, by the way."

Ynya smiled, but the girl never met her gaze long enough to notice.

Something had happened to that girl. She once had the spark of hope, but it had been taken out of her by those horrible people out there.

More rage boiled to the surface, but Ynya tamped it back down. She shouldn't test her cage quite yet.

She turned to study the environment she was in. The cell was large, allowing six to eight people to sit on the bench along the back wall. A single torch on the wall shed enough light to navigate the short hallway.

The hallway ended in a solid iron door, with three other barred cells in the room.

There wasn't much to go off of, but it looked like if she figured out how to get the bars melted for this cell, Ynya might be able to get everyone into the hallway and prepared for when the guards came. As long as they could use the magic in the hallway, they would be fine.

"Well, if you're not going to do something, I'm going to do it."

She poured heat into the bars.

Chapter Twenty-Three

The steel door at the end of the hallway slammed open, and the woman in black strode in.

"Ynya Oblique, are we going to have any issues here?"

Ynya removed her hands from the barely heated metal.

Damn, that was too fast. There is no way she was just waiting outside the room to come bursting in, was she?

The woman stopped just outside of the cell, so close that her clothes brushed the outside of the bars. She brandished the silver blade once again, twirling it in her hands. "You may want to take a step back unless I decide I want to use this on you again."

Ynya took a step forward. Audible gasps filled the cell, the prisoners shocked that someone stood up to the guards here. Ynya didn't care. Staying in here and giving up to tyranny was the only way to lose. As long as she stood her ground, she was winning.

The woman paused for a moment, then smiled. Her teeth were perfectly straight and white, something Ynya hadn't noticed before.

"How many tents burned down?" Ynya asked, winking at the woman who was an inch shorter than her.

The woman's eyebrows twitched. She spun the blade once more and it disappeared in a flash under one of her leather flaps.

"Too many. You impress me, Ynya Oblique. I sense powerful magic in you, but I'm unable to pinpoint exactly what type. Normally this comes quite easy for me, but with you, it's an enigma."

She cocked her head to the side to look at the metal where Ynya's hands had just been. Her eyes flicked to Ynya's for a moment before she spun and spoke.

"It's no matter. Once you go to Reyoarfjell, we will know more about you than you do yourself."

"Oh yeah, how so?"

The woman waved her hand across the whole cell. "You all have what, one, possibly two powers? Heat, cold, wind, maybe even earth magic? Our interrogators at Reyoarfjell have the ability to find out powers you didn't know you had."

The room turned silent.

"You didn't know this? And here you thought hedge witches wielded two kinds of powers, three at the most?" She clucked her tongue while taking a step, her tight leather clothes creaking as she walked.

"Oh no, you have so, so much more to give to your Queen, and she has figured out how to take it; she has figured out how you can best serve her. You will be molded, shaped, and changed into whatever she needs you to be."

She stopped pacing and moved so fast Ynya could swear she teleported. "But you, Ynya. You are special, and I suspect your sister is special, too."

Ynya tensed. She was the only one of her family, other

than her mother, who had any magic. At least her two younger sisters hadn't shown any magic yet.

The woman smiled. "I can hear your brain trying to puzzle things out, trying to come up with reasons why I would be speaking about this. You see, magic is usually passed down through bloodlines, mother to daughter, father to son. Rarely, if the stars align, and the moon is just right, a baby can be born with magic, thus starting a new bloodline.

"So I have to wonder, Ynya Oblique, does your sister have magic?"

"My sister?"

The woman pouted. "Don't think I don't know about the little arrangement your brother-in-law's family has with Her Majesty."

"My sister doesn't have magic."

"Hmm." The reply was a high-pitched sound, almost like a mouse squeak.

Ynya's blood boiled once again. She was sick of these games. She wanted to burn something. She wanted to punch this woman in the face.

Instead she chose to verbally jab, and the words just poured out of her. "You know who did have magic? My mother, but your soldiers didn't capture her for the Queen, oh no. They had other plans, plans of their own." Ynya grabbed the bars in front of her, pouring heat into them so fast they began to glow.

"They stabbed her to death so she bled out in the snow, then proceeded to rape her corpse. They didn't even try to capture her for the glory of your precious Frost Queen, they slaughtered her. Your troops are so stupid and undisciplined that they overlooked the only other mage in the entire village because they were too bloodthirsty to know better."

The woman leaned forward, her forehead nearly fitting between the bars. Her voice was low and careful. "Careful, Ynya, or I might have to make an example of you. You know I can't look weak in front of the prisoners."

Ynya released her grasp of the bars. Terrified gasps came from the rest of the cell. She only hoped it breathed some semblance of fight in them. She needed their help if she was going to get out of this place.

The woman in leather pursed her lips, a slight look of concern on her face. Wrinkled formed on her forehead. "So your mother is dead? That should not have happened."

"What, the murder or the rape? Or do your soldiers even know the difference?"

She received an angry glare in reply.

Good. I'm getting to her.

The woman spoke, but her voice was strained, like she was holding back from saying what she truly felt. "It will be investigated and punished, I assure you."

She spun. "Guards!"

The door at the end of the hall slammed open once again and two burly soldiers stepped in. "Captain Nora?"

"Prepare for departure. We leave at first light."

"Yes, ma'am."

"Oh, and take the sister along. If this one has magic, there is a chance the sister has it as well. They will find out."

Ynya opened her mouth to speak but the woman rushed at her in a blur and stabbed her three more times with the silver blade. "Uh uh uh, little girl. You need to learn your place, and your place is not to speak right now."

Ynya crumpled to the floor, hitting her head against the bars on the way down.

"Pleasant dreams."

The woman walked down the hall and slammed the iron door at the end.

As the metallic sound echoed through the room, Ynya realized her mistake once again. She'd given too much away. The remark about her mother now meant that her sister would be taken. Her effort to show how strong and capable she was backfired once again, but this time it didn't just affect her own safety, now it affected her sister, and the baby.

All Ynya had to do was keep her mouth shut and they would have left without Synol. She slumped to the floor, all the heat and rage dissipating and replaced with regret.

Smoke, not fire.

Tears poured down her face at her mistake. "I'm sorry, Synol."

Chapter Twenty-Four

Ynya fell asleep on the floor.

She dreamed of coming back to her village, finding her sister, bleeding on the ground in the same location her mama had died. Blood pooled between Synol's legs. Her tears were the only thing that moved, falling to the ground with a splash, the rest of the world frozen in time.

Ynya woke with a start when the guard clanged his wooden baton on the hard metal bars.

"Up and at 'em! We're taking you north."

The woman in black, Captain Nora, watched with mild ambivalence as the prisoners were loaded into the back of a metal barred wagon. The top and bottom were thick wood, so setting them on fire would do nothing but burn up the rest of the group inside her wagon.

Ynya didn't feel like fighting this morning. She complied, falling into line with the rest of the captured mages and shuffling along in arm and leg irons.

As she passed by Captain Nora, the woman in black scoffed, reminding Ynya of her place and how easy it was to manipulate her into giving her the exact information she came to seek.

All six mages shuffled into the cart, and the soldiers bolted a thick door of bars behind them.

Captain Nora addressed the entire wagon while her uncomfortable gaze never left Ynya. "I trust you all will be obedient on our journey. I would hate to have to get angry."

One of the guards banged on the bars twice, and the wagon lurched forward.

They met with other wagons in the town square, one of which held a half dozen kids and an old woman with burned eyes.

"Oh no." Ynya's heart broke as she watched the kids holding onto the bars, their dirty faces filling up the space between the metal.

"What?" Joanne asked.

"I know those kids, I know that woman. She helped hide me for a few days. I don't know how they got caught." A thought entered her mind. "I hope it wasn't something I did."

Ynya looked over at the wagon, catching the eye of one of the kids. She mouthed 'I'm sorry' but the little boy simply stared back, a blank expression like he'd already given up.

Her life had gone from amazing to terrifying in just a few days, but now it was even worse. She'd spent a scant few hours with anyone in this town and already everyone she'd met was being taken by the soldiers to Reyoarfjell.

She looked up at the looming manor of the Torkelsen Estate as two barn doors at the base opened up.

From underneath, a covered wagon trotted out, followed by Stefan on horseback.

"Do you know what that's about?" Firtz asked her.

"It's my sister. They are taking her too."

There didn't seem to be any bars on the windows, and the door to the wagon wasn't locked. Ynya hoped her sister wasn't in irons because of her. Ynya might have gotten her captured, but she hoped she didn't get her sister tortured. Ynya wouldn't be able to forgive herself if Synol were harmed because of her actions.

The caravan stopped for a while at the camp north of town.

Along the way, Ynya got to know the other mages in the wagon. Hans and Joanne were both in their twenties and had grown up around this area.

Firtz had been a blacksmith his entire life and swore up and down he didn't know magic, but she didn't miss the wink and smile he gave her as he insisted he was innocently abducted.

Tyrain, a twelve-year-old boy, had accidentally sneezed one day at dinner, causing a gust of wind to lift all dresses in the entire hall over the women's heads.

"I swear I wasn't trying to do that!" But all the men chuckled anyway.

At least spirits are slightly up. It is something.

Midway through the day, they stopped again, and everyone was let out to stretch their legs while the soldiers prepared a broth-like meal for everyone to drink.

The woman in black was nowhere to be found.

"Hey, where did she go?" asked Ynya.

Joanne sidled up to her and spoke in a low voice. "I saw her veer off at the encampment to one of the tents. I don't think she joined back up with us after that."

"You cannot already be thinking about escape?" Hans asked.

"I just want to know where she is. The rest of us can take

any of the guards, but she's the one to watch out for. If she's gone for even a couple of hours, we might be able to get out of here, and more importantly, get those kids out of here. It's my fault they are here, I have to help them escape."

Hans kicked at a small mound of snow. "I don't think we should be doing this."

Joanne whirled on him. "I know we shouldn't be doing this, but here we are. You've heard the stories of what happens to mages at Reyoarfjell. I'd rather die in the snow then be taken there and dissected."

Ynya nodded, as did others.

Hans sighed. "I hear if you cooperate, they go lenient on you, and give you a solid job with meals and lodging."

Ynya jutted her chin at the wagon full of non-magical children. "What about them? None of them have magic, but since they're all siblings to someone who does, or kids of parents, they're going to be tortured until some magic comes out."

So will Synol.

"I can't allow that to happen, I just can't. If you want to stay back, I won't fault you. I will go at this alone, but if any of you are willing, I could use the help."

Firtz spoke up, reluctant to admit his magical talent out loud. "I can heat up the metal just like you, lass."

"Good. Do you think we can get rid of these shackles without burning anyone here?"

Hans sighed, clearly exasperated at the conversation. "I can keep our wrists from building up too much heat."

"Frost mage?"

"No, but I can create barriers that prevent things from passing, so I can keep the heat from getting to people's skin and burning them."

"If we do this now, before they put us back into the wagon, we're going to have a better shot of it." Ynya caught the gaze of every mage there. "We all ready?"

She got an affirmative nod from everyone but Hans, who finally rolled his eyes and agreed.

Ynya and the blacksmith poured massive amounts of heat into their own shackles. The smell of hot metal filled the wagon, as if they forged weapons to gain their freedom.

Chapter Twenty-Five

❧

"Guard!" Joanne hissed.

All the mages huddled together close to the back of the wagon, forming a wall around Ynya and Firtz so they could continue working their magic.

The guard eyed the group of mages huddled around each other. "You lot about done here?"

Joanne nodded. "Yeah, but I think my shackles are starting to come loose here. You better check them."

He looked at her suspiciously.

She laughed. "What are you afraid of? If any of us try anything, that scary black-haired bitch is going to be on us in a second, right? We learned our lesson after watching red-hair over here mouth off to her. Right, all?"

The rest of the mages nodded. Ynya's shackles softened. If she pulled right now she could stretch them out, but she required more room and would probably be noticed. They needed to get rid of the guard.

Instead, he walked closer. "Yeah, that's a lesson you all

better learn early right? There is nowhere you can be safe. She's always watching."

Joanne held out her hands and shook them. "See?"

Interestingly enough, her hands did seem abnormally small in those cuffs. Just as the guard got up to her, she yanked her hands out of the cuffs and clapped him on the head, just as Hans projected a barrier around the man's mouth to dampen any noise.

Ynya's shackles fell to the ground, and she turned to free Hans from his.

Joanne grabbed the key just as the blacksmith finished getting his off and unlocked more.

With all of them freed, the mages took up defensive positions behind the wagon to scope out the soldiers.

"Three up above patrolling, one behind, and two are putting away the food. We don't have much time." Joanne said.

Ynya nodded. "We have enough for everyone to take out one guard each. Then we can use the caravan to get everyone here to safety. We're going to need to coordinate attacks though, take them by surprise as much as we can all at once so they can't call for reinforcements."

"Well, thank you much for the help, ladies, but I'm going my own way." Hans took a step to the north.

"Where do you think you're going?" Ynya asked.

He stopped and turned. "I didn't want to go along with this plan, but the plan has been executed, regardless. I wish nothing but good luck to you, but I'm saving myself."

The boy Tyrain spoke up. "I'm going with him as well."

Two more nods came from the group of mages.

Ynya felt her blood boil once again. "Are you kidding

me? I just helped you all escape, and you can't spare one minute to help us take out the rest of the guards?"

Hans shrugged. "I appreciate the help, but running is the only thing you can do. Start and never stop. I might need that minute." He clapped Tyrain on the shoulder. "Let's go."

The two mages ran, followed by two more of the small group.

Ynya, Firtz, and Joanne watched them go before Joanne shrugged and turned toward the camp.

"We could still take out the guards, but it's going to be a bit of a struggle."

"Where did the guards go?" Firtz pointed to where the two had been putting out the food.

"Oh no." Ynya heard the whistle of air for a split second before something smashed into her back.

Beside her, Joanna grunted before falling to the snow.

The blacksmith whirled, shooting flames out of his hand at the soldier who was about to attack him, but he was too late to stop the attack entirely. The large wooden club came down on the blacksmith's nose with a sickening crunch.

Ynya rolled, her back spasming from the blow, and kicked out, trying to catch the guard.

But the guard moved quickly, taking one step backward to ensure he didn't get tripped by her legs. He swung again, aiming at her knee. She rolled to the side and his club hit the ground with a thud.

Joanne lay in a heap on the ground, the blacksmith's face was bloody, and Ynya's back hurt like it was broken.

Heal!

Her body had always healed faster than anyone else she'd known. Mama had told her it was due to her heat, but Ynya suspected it had more to do with her mother's healing abilities. Ynya had never managed to heal herself from broken bones while lying at the bottom of a glacier crevasse quite like she could in the warmth and care of her Mama.

Ynya grabbed a handful of snow and tossed it at the man's face. He dodged, but it gave her enough time to stand and run.

As she passed him by, he tried to elbow her. He missed, sending him spinning in place for a half-second.

It was enough time for Ynya to grab him by the neck and pour heat into his body. She needed to knock him out and get back to helping the others. Ynya held on with all she could muster, and in a few seconds the man stopped batting at her.

Another guard came up behind her and pelted her in the back with a club, knocking the wind out of her and lancing pain through her spine.

Ynya let go and fell to the floor in agony. She screamed as her back spasmed. She watched in slow-motion as the soldier fell on top of her, every detail playing out for her.

I'm done for.

We're all done for.

Ynya hoped the other mages had at least made it to safety.

She was yanked backwards, out from under the unconscious soldier atop her. It wasn't a guard who pulled her out, however.

It was Hans. His lips pressed into a worried and concentrated line.

"Get up, we have to go right now."

Chapter Twenty-Six

P ain pulsed through Ynya's back, but she stumbled to her feet. Her vision wobbled around her, like her brain still wasn't able to process everyone else's movements. She wavered for a few seconds, trying to get her bearings.

Hans held three guards at bay with some kind of invisible field. Tyrain held Joanne under her arms, dragging her limp body through the snow. The two other mages who had run off with Hans were gone, but the blacksmith wielded two clubs in his hands.

"You all right?" Hans asked her. "We have to go."

Ynya nodded, her mind still addled by the recent attack. She took a step then another, and another. Bolstered by nerves, magic, or something else, each movement lessened the pain, and soon she wasn't stumbling anymore.

"Keep moving, it will help you get your bearings."

Ynya nodded. It was helping.

The five made their way out of the camp toward the north, keeping up with the pace of Tyrain as he dragged Joanne's limp body.

Every now and again Firtz launched an attack at one of the soldiers, getting in one or two good shots with either his clubs or a fire attack.

Ynya watched in rapt amazement at his ability to shoot fire from his hands. She'd never managed to figure out how to do it herself. It must just be his special ability. She felt safer with him around, a mature mage who understood the value of human life and had the experience to back up his abilities.

She felt a little better and moved over to help the boy carry Joanne.

But as she did, she looked to see everyone watching from the caravan. The two other wagons carrying prisoners stuck in her mind. All the small non-magic children huddled in their cages, their little eyes glued on her movements.

But the one that finally got to her was seeing Synol standing in the doorway of her covered carriage. She wore no shackles, she had no cuffs, but she was just as much a prisoner as the rest of them. She was due for the same exact fate.

Ynya's heart broke. Yet again she'd rushed into something without a proper plan and others paid the price.

No more.

She couldn't blame the mages for looking out for themselves. They had only their best interests in mind. None of them had gotten an entire wagon full of small children locked up and sent to the horrors unknown.

None of them had outed her own mother as a mage in an attempt to feel better about herself and prove just how tough she was to another mage.

Her own hubris and inability to keep her mouth shut had brought suspicion on her own sister. And even though Stefan's father had most likely turned in the location of her family, he did it with the intention of keeping his son's new wife safe from the Frost Queen's clutches.

At least they were trying, even if it meant collateral damage.

All Ynya did was leave a wake of destruction in her path.

She didn't deserve freedom, but the rest of them did. After all of this, if she didn't at least save Synol, then what would it have been good for? She came here to recover her sisters, and now she was escaping with mages she'd barely met less than a day ago.

She dropped Joanne. "Take her."

"What are you doing?" Hans asked.

"What I came here to do. You all keep running, I'll make sure you are able to escape." Ynya looked at the blacksmith, then nodded in the direction of the guard who limped and was bloodied from his last attack.

Firtz grimaced and nodded.

Ynya ran. Two of the guards followed her, and the blacksmith yelled a deep guttural roar. She heard the crunch of bone and the grunt as the guard crumpled to the snow.

At least they'll make it out.

She kept running, making sure to slow her escape just enough to keep the guards on her. She glanced over her shoulder, noticing the guard in the snow and four mages gone.

Good.

Ynya turned back toward the camp and picked up the pace. She wove through the horses and dodged a guard who popped out, trying to grab her.

She ran past the wagon with the orphans, and yelled at Miss-Miss. "I will get you all out, I promise!"

The slight hint of a nod caught her eye as she sprinted past, toward the middle of the caravan.

"Synol!"

Her sister looked up, still standing inside her carriage. She had a sour look on her face and wasn't wearing her furs. She clearly hadn't been planning on making a run for it and was more comfortable lounging inside her rolling prison.

Ynya's mind raced. If she grabbed Synol right now she would have to find warm clothes for her sister. They would have to run through the snow too, and as she rounded the corner, she saw her sister's bare feet.

Dammit!

This wouldn't work. She couldn't grab her sister right now. There was no way they would make it.

Ynya's mind raced, trying to find any other solution, but none came. Grabbing a horse with three guards on her tail was a stupid move. Trying to convince Stefan to take his barefoot pregnant bride through the snow with no clothes wouldn't work either.

Ynya couldn't even get the orphans out.

She was done for.

Ynya skidded to a stop next to Synol's carriage, locking her gaze on her sister's face and pleading with her eyes that Synol would somehow volunteer to run.

"Synol, please we need to go find Finny and Meki. You see what they are doing to us here."

But of course Synol didn't. She frowned, and crossed her arms on her chest. She wasn't moving.

"Mama and Papa mollified you too much, Ynya. It's time to grow up and face the consequences for your childish antics."

"I agree." The woman's voice came from the side.

Ynya's stomach clenched as she recognized the clear, sharp voice.

She turned to watch the woman in black leather striding towards her through the snow, tossing the silver knife in her hands.

"You were here the whole time?" Ynya asked.

Captain Nora smiled. "I wanted to see how good you all were, get an idea of what I dealt with. I have to say I'm rather surprised at the lack of planning." She tsk'd her tongue a few times, then turned to Synol. "So, big sister, you know her best. How do we contain her?"

Synol furrowed her brow, giving a quick glance to Ynya then back to the woman. "It's simple. Put her some place warm and well-insulated. My cabin will do nicely. She will overheat and not be able to do anything."

Chapter Twenty-Seven

Ynya woke. She was wrapped entirely in blankets. She was also shackled with a thick chain strapped to her ankles, wrists, and waist.

She wanted to melt them off, but the blankets around her trapped too much heat and caused her to black out.

She had learned that the hard way already.

"You really should stop struggling, Ynya." Synol frowned from her seat across from Ynya.

"If you just undo these blankets, I'll be able to get the two of us out of here."

Synol leaned back in her seat. "You know I cannot." She looked over at the nurse Edith who was also in there with them. "You see what I have to deal with? She's the main reason I left my old life."

Edith nodded, a slight smile on her face.

The steady sound of Stefan's horse bore into Ynya's mind. The ever-present clomp clomp clomp that never left the carriage's side. It was what drove her to try to escape the last time.

And of course Captain Nora wasn't far behind, sticking her nose into the carriage from time to time.

"I read the document, Synol. I know what they are doing. They only married you to get to us."

Synol turned up her nose. "I'm not talking about this with you. Stefan loves me."

"It doesn't matter if he does or not. The only thing that matters is the family. They killed Mama and Papa and kidnapped Finny and Meki. Now you and I are chained and being taken to the same place."

Synol shifted her legs, crossing them one way then again the other way. Finally, she crossed her arms. "I'm not shackled, because I'm following the rules, something you can't seem to do."

As the heat rose once again around Ynya, she had to take some slow breaths to calm herself down. She couldn't afford to overheat, not again. She needed to keep her temper under control to stay awake and alert.

"Fine, I have been a bad girl, and I will take whatever punishment I deserve for my many crimes, whatever those are."

Synol huffed. "Whatever those are? They say that you are the one who set fire to our town. When they came to arrest you, you killed soldiers and ran. They have been chasing you ever since."

Ynya's mind raced as worry replaced rage in her mind. "Is that what they've told you? Is that–" Her voice broke at the thought. Hot tears flowed down her face and soaked into the blankets. "Do you think I killed Mama? Do you think I could possibly hurt Papa?"

The normal heat in her skin chilled in a heartbeat.

How can my sister think I'm capable of such horrors?

Synol turned away, her eyes flushing with tears. For a moment the tension seemed to pause as the carriage bumped down the road. The moment dragged on for an awful time as both girls dealt with their own rush of emotions.

Despite her horror at the realization, Ynya's heartbeat was strangely slow and calm now that all the unspoken thoughts had been aired.

"Synol, you know me. You know I may be reckless, I may have been mollified as you said, I may be childish, but I never put anyone in any danger that I wasn't willing to put myself in. You also know I would never hurt anyone in our village."

She wished so much to reach her hand out and touch her sister. She wanted any human contact at that moment.

"I was out on a solo fishing trip and came back to the carnage. You must believe me. I don't care what else you think, you have to know I would never do something like that."

Synol turned, wiping away the tears. "I don't know what else to think, Ynya. I don't know what I'm doing here half the time."

"Why are you here? Why did you come?"

"Captain Nora said I needed to come to testify on your behalf at a trial...help be your defense...which I jumped at, you know. Nothing is more important—"

"—than family." The two girls finished the phrase together.

"Synol, they have lied to you, I saw the document myself in the office on the second floor. I had it in my pocket until they arrested me."

Ynya looked out of the windows to ensure Stefan wasn't within earshot. She lowered her voice just in case.

"Ask your husband if it's true. His father made a deal

with the Frost Queen to know of our existence, your hand for our location. I know all about the fake names and location, but I've spoken to someone who was actually from Kropprfjell and she says the city was burned to the ground tens of years ago. The only people who were from there still alive are scarred and at least seventy years old by now.

"I want you to think carefully. Even if you don't care about my fate, you must care about Finny and Meki. What is to become of them?"

Synol sighed and looked out the window. Her eyes went wide and her nostrils flared.

Ynya glanced out the window. Stefan rode there once again, but so did his father. How she hadn't noticed the gaunt old man in the caravan up to this point was beyond her.

After another quick glance out the window, Synol spoke. Her face was emotionless and tense. "I do care about them, but there are rules and protocols to follow for a civilized society, Ynya. You just need to let me handle things on my own terms. You get all hot headed and break the rules and other people pay for it. If you had just played the games like Mama told you, you wouldn't be in this mess."

The men rode side by side, but this time the father was the one closer to the carriage.

They were eavesdropping. Most likely the nurse was as well, but Ynya couldn't worry about her now. She wouldn't be able to tell anyone else until they stopped and got out, so now, the girls just needed to play along.

Ynya decided to break the silence with banter expected of women.

"Do you remember pulling taffy in the spring?"

Synol smiled ever so slightly. "Coating our hands in

butter and holding onto it just long enough until it burned us? Well, not you of course, but the rest of us would dance around trying to keep the taffy moving fast enough so it didn't harden."

"Mama yelling the whole time to not let it touch the floor."

"If Ynya can do it with her eyes closed, you girls can do with your eyes open!"

For the first time since the girls had seen each other, and possibly in the last four years, Synol actually giggled at the memory.

"Stuffing Meki's pants so full of dirt that she couldn't fall over."

"I did that to Finny too, but you might have been too young to remember."

"Mama wasn't happy."

"Papa sure laughed though, told Mama to leave her so she could rest for once."

The two laughed out loud at the situation. Tension in the carriage dissipated with each genuine laugh, and Ynya felt like she had her sister back. The two hadn't had such a good relationship since—

"Venturing into Yolphinir's cave and nearly getting ourselves killed."

Synol stopped laughing and frowned.

Ynya realized her mistake as soon as the words left her mouth. Regret and worry washed over her as she tried to diffuse the situation. "I'm sorry. I shouldn't have brought that up."

The two rode in an uncomfortable silence for a while. Ynya remembered how her mother taught her to focus her mind, concentrating on certain thoughts or memories and pushing out the others. It was a way to handle stressful situations, but hadn't been one Ynya had to use much.

The silence between the two grew and gnawed, and despite all the focusing exercises, Ynya couldn't take it any longer.

"Is that where it all went wrong between us?"

Synol turned away, her lips drawn to a fine, colorless line.

"I never thought there would be a frost bear in the cave. If I had known–"

"It's always 'if I had known' with you, Ynya. Always regretting but never learning."

"Are you two done reminiscing?" Captain Nora stood in the open doorway of the carriage, having snuck in when the two weren't looking. "It's time for a demonstration."

Captain Nora grabbed Ynya, blankets shackles and all, and lifted her out of the door and atop the carriage in a single motion. The woman was scarily strong.

Wind howled from the north in front of them, cooling down Ynya's overheated body. She had been managing her body temperature well enough inside the carriage, but now that she was outside, she might be able to take out one chain at a time as long as the wind continue to blow like it did.

If she pushed excess body heat through her scalp and into her hair, but not enough for it to glow, it would dissipate even faster. She did just that, dumping as much as she could without attracting attention.

"What is going on?" Synol asked, shivering through the biting cold. The nurse popped below to grab a blanket for her mistress.

Ynya eyed the nurse, wondering if she was going to go spill everything they'd talked about to the guards.

"Oh, just a small lesson for you and your sister." Captain Nora whistled. In the distance, a form stood up from the snow and jogged toward them.

It was the woman in white, the woman with the frost bear pelt for clothes.

Ynya had wondered if she too was Skarmyord, but she supposed she had her answer now.

Ynya's heart sank. She now had two of them following her. One was bad enough.

She glanced behind her, taking in the two prison wagons. One was still empty, meaning the other mages hadn't been caught yet.

Good.

The other was still full of orphans and Miss-Miss. None of them had protection from the cold. Out here on the plains, the wind gusted to dreadful levels, and without any protection from the biting frozen rain, the children would lose arms, feet, or die.

"Don't worry, I won't let them freeze to death tonight. They aren't any use to us if we let them die." Captain Nora had followed her gaze. "Your friends have managed to slip our grasp for now, but that is nothing to worry about. Out here in the frozen wilderness, there isn't anywhere to hide. They will have to go to a town eventually, and as you know, both towns they could travel to are heavily guarded by my men."

Ynya looked away. "If you put me in with the orphans, I promise to keep them warm and not run."

The Captain huffed. "It is possible you might keep your word. But you have been a slippery one, Ynya Oblique, and keeping you with your sister seems like the more prudent thing to do now."

"I'm not leaving without her."

"I agree, but I still cannot take chances. You have to understand how things are from my perspective. Failure to bring you in reflects badly upon me and my skills. Ahh, here we are."

The woman in white furs arrived at the caravan, and in a single leap, jumped to the top of the carriage, landing so lightly that the whole structure barely shook from her weight.

Ynya remembered the light footprints the woman left in the snow alongside the road. The memory caused a shiver to go down her spine.

"I believe you two have already met?"

Ynya grimaced, but the woman in white smiled a pleasant, sultry smile.

"We go way back."

Nora pointed into the snow.

"As you girls certainly know, there are rabbits in these plains. Kalda here is going to show you just how deadly the Skarmyord can be."

"You're trying to scare us?"

"I'm trying to educate you. Your sister, bless her soul, is trying to help you, Ynya. She's trying to help you understand how your actions affect others. I'm here to put an exclamation point on the end of her lesson. Kalda?"

Kalda produced a bow from beneath her fur, and three arrows followed.

Three shiny black arrows.

Ynya payed close attention.

Kalda crept forward to the corner of the carriage and scanned the horizon.

"I see seven groups of rabbits. How many should I take down?"

"One group will work for tonight. We don't have many mouths to feed. The guards will appreciate a nice hot meal. Five should do."

Kalda nodded and blinked a few times into the constantly howling wind from the north.

Underneath the blankets, Ynya superheated the shackle on her left ankle to the point where she was able to get two fingers in there and pull her ankle out at the next gust of wind. One down, four to go.

"There." Kalda drew back her bow, nocked one arrow and held the other two in her hand. In a flurry of movement, she unleashed three arrows back to back so fast, it looked to Ynya to be just one blurry arrow shot.

Twang, twang, twang!

All three shots sounded so close together it would have been easy to mistake it for one single shot, but Ynya counted each one, distinct from the next.

She needed to know how good Kalda was with those arrows. She needed to pay back for Hvarf's grisly death.

"Got them?"

Kalda rolled her eyes. "Take a guess." She leaped off the caravan, launching herself into the air a solid ten feet vertically and landing on the snow at least twenty feet out. Still, she barely made the carriage creak.

I better hurry, I won't be out here much longer.

Ynya poured as much heat as she could muster into the next leg iron. She was just able to slip it off as Kalda showed back up from the darkness holding three arrows. Two of them had a single rabbit on them, while the third arrow had three smaller ones.

Nora pouted. "And here I thought you were going to impress us."

"You told me five."

"That I did. Guards! Get the cooking pot going, we have fresh meat for the crew!"

She turned to Ynya, who concentrated on her left wrist shackle right now. "You see, dear, we Skarmyord are quite well trained, each with our own unique skills. Kalda here managed to kill five rabbits with three arrows in unfamiliar terrain, looking into the setting sun with a massive cross-wind. I hope you understand just how precarious your position is here."

Ynya smiled and nodded as she slipped the third shackle from her wrist.

"I understand perfectly."

Chapter Twenty-Eight

Synol headed down first, giving Ynya a precious few more seconds to loosen the final band on her hands, leaving just the one around her waist.

She was starting to work on the final one when Nora grabbed her by her hair.

"I see steam coming off your hair, young one. Is there something I need to know?"

Ynya rattled the chains underneath her blankets. They were all just barely loose enough that she could pull her limbs out of them, but other than a close inspection, it shouldn't be obvious.

"Don't worry, I'm not going anywhere. I can't help it, I've been on the verge of overheating in that stuffy cabin. You're the one who brought me out here, so don't blame me if I'm cooling off from the wind."

Nora eyed her for a moment before glancing down at Ynya's feet in the shackles.

"Am I going to get dinner like the rest? I did get injured

by your guards today. You wouldn't want me to fall ill and die, would you?"

Nora let go of Ynya's hair, then pulled back and slapped her with the back of her hand.

Pain shot through Ynya's jaw, and she flew backward off the carriage and landed on her head in the snow.

Despite the reaction, Ynya pushed more heat into the middle part around her torso, fingers from her hands pulling with all her might to overheat the metal as fast as she could and allow her enough room to slip out of the iron.

"You need to learn to be more respectful."

Nora grabbed the chains between Ynya's legs, which thankfully had fallen up to her knees, and tugged them, flipping Ynya back to a sitting position. "Throw her back in without any dinner."

Captain Nora stormed away, not noticing the bare patch of melted earth where Ynya's head and hair had been.

"You shouldn't push her so much, Ynya." Synol pulled grass and leaves from her hair as Ynya tried to get herself situated once again.

Now was the time. The guards were all busy getting dinner ready, the ever-present Torkelsen men were nowhere to be seen. Even the nurse was gone.

"Synol, I have one more thing to tell you before they get back." Ynya whispered, hoping one of the abilities of the Skarmyord wasn't amazing hearing.

"What?"

"You know how we always talked about what magic Mama had?"

Synol's eyebrows knitted together and she looked at the door.

"It's all right, they're all gone, but do you remember?"

"Of course," Synol hissed through clenched teeth. She stood partially up and glanced through one side of the carriage windows.

"She gave me her power, Synol."

"What?" Synol pulled the drapes shut and whirled around. Her eyes were wild and crazed, like she had gone feral. "She *what*?"

"I told you she waited there for two days in the frozen ground, but she was alive, Synol. She waited for me to give me her power."

"Well?" Synol went to the other side of the carriage to peer out those windows.

"Well what?"

"What was it? Healing? Weather prediction? Glamours?"

Ynya shook her head. "I don't know."

"What! How can you not know?"

"I don't know, alright? She pushed this power into me. I can feel but I don't know how to use it."

Synol rolled her eyes.

"Look, you don't have magic, and you don't know how this all works. That's fine, but I'm telling you, once you have bloomed, you just learn to live with it. You naturally figure out how to use it. Having magic is like having hands. You don't ever think about how it might be strange or different that you have it, you just do.

"I don't ever remember figuring out how light up my hair, I just always knew how. It's the same as walking or breathing or pissing in the snow. You just always know. I don't know what Mama's power is because I have only had it a few days and I haven't been able to test it yet."

Synol gave Ynya a look of incredulity, but then her face softened.

"I suppose you haven't had enough time to see if you can predict the weather, have you?"

Ynya shook her head. She wondered if she should tell Synol about her shackles but decided to keep that one to herself for now.

Synol continued. "I was always leaning toward weather myself. The way she knew when to tell father to head out on his fishing trips or when to come home was uncanny."

"I thought it was gardening, personally."

Synol glanced away, looking out the window again. "Why gardening?"

"You know how good our garden was in the greenhouse. She managed to keep things growing like it was summer all year long."

"I think that was more to do with intellect than magic. Putting up the glass was just smart. It kept the heat in all winter long. She could have accomplished the same thing by just having you live in the room full-time, but you refused to stay inside for more than a few minutes."

Ynya snorted as a memory bubbled up through her recollection.

"What's so funny?" Synol looked out over the other window.

"Maybe it was magic over Papa. Remember how he would come home from fishing, grab us all in a big bear hug, then put us down and say 'Girls, I haven't seen your mother in a long time, we have much to discuss.'"

Synol smiled, a warm, genuine smile Ynya hadn't seen in such a long time. "Mama would give us a dirty look if we didn't clear out immediately."

"I know!" Ynya yelled louder than she had meant to. Thoughts of her current situation fled her mind. She was in the moment, in the memories, of her family. "We couldn't go back to that yurt for hours!"

"Or keeping Meki from interrupting them."

Ynya's eyes went wide as a realization came to her.

"What?" Synol asked, concern in her voice.

"I finally realized why they kicked us out." Her face went bright red as heated blood flooded her skin. "Oh no!"

Synol sat back down, her face beet red too, as the two girls devolved into a restrained giggle.

Chapter Twenty-Nine

I t was early in the morning when Ynya woke up to the caustic twinge of burnt timber.

Craning her neck, she tried to see outside in the morning light, but sitting on the floor of the carriage she was only able to see sky. Not wanting to risk being found with loose bonds, she had fallen asleep to the gentle rocking while waiting for the right time to escape.

Now, the sky was cloudy and blue in the early morning light.

Synol was awake, staring out the window.

"What do you see?" Ynya recognized the awful smell of burned wood, pitch, and bodies.

Synol looked over at her sister for a second, then back out the window. In that brief moment of time, Ynya verified all the information she needed.

They were definitely outside Marsfjord.

Ynya softened her voice, not wanting to preach, but simply to punctuate an existing thought.

"You know it wasn't me that burned down the village.

Other than when I was a young girl and was still learning to control my powers, I've never set fire to anything I didn't want."

Synol nodded, tears streaking down her face.

Ynya opened her mouth to speak, but didn't know what to say. Sometimes, silence was the only appropriate response. She had to remind herself she'd spent a couple days here tending to the dead, hoping they would find some semblance of peace in the afterlife.

For Synol, this was all new. She hadn't seen it with her own eyes, and she needed to grieve in her own way.

Ynya watched as tears streamed down her sister's cheek. Each one reached her chin and dripped off onto her blanket. Synol made a fist. Slowly, she released it, stretching out each individual finger, cracking a couple knuckles, then went back to a fist.

Ynya hadn't remembered Synol doing something so unladylike as cracking her bones in years. It was refreshing to know the sister she had grown up with and looked up to all those years was still in there, buried beneath the quagmire of adult relationships and unwritten rules for the wealthy elite.

As Synol pumped her hand, Ynya felt her heartbeat slow to match her sister's motion. It was a calm, steady beat. A comfortable groove.

"They could have just taken–" Synol stopped abruptly and looked at Ynya, a stricken look on her face.

"Just taken me?" Ynya nodded. "I know. I wish that's what they did. I wish they had just taken me and let the rest go. I would give anything to have not gone on that fishing trip, given anything to be there so I could help defend their lives."

Ynya thought back to the day she left. She remembered

the clouds in the sky. She had been worried about the storm, but her mother promised her everything was going to be alright.

She'd even insisted that it was the correct time to leave. She had insisted that Ynya go right then in fact...

Ynya sat bolt upright.

"What is it?"

"I think Mama knew."

"Knew? Knew what?"

"I think she knew the soldiers were coming."

Synol's eyes widened, and her mouth drew to a hard line. "What do you mean?"

"Storm clouds were coming in from the north, and even Papa worried about me going alone, but Mama insisted I leave, in fact, she help load the boat herself."

"Mama never does that, that's always Papa's chore."

Ynya nodded. "I know. She told me to hurry, even though I had the whole day to leave. Now I have to wonder if she knew something was coming and wanted me out of there before the soldiers came. Maybe she hoped that if I was gone, the soldiers would check the village and move on."

"But how would she know?"

The two sisters stared blankly at each other for a moment. The normal tension between them had changed to a static charge, building as the two sorted out the puzzle that was their mother.

"That's quite strange." Synol said, looking out the window once again.

"What do you mean?" Ynya wished she could see out of the window, but then remembered she'd seen the image too many times. She knew exactly what the village graveyard, looked like. Perhaps it was best they spoke like this, it kept the emotions and anger at bay.

"Why would Mama load your boat? Do you think she put something in there?"

Realization hit Ynya and she opened her mouth to say, but at that moment the door opened up, and Synol's nurse came back in.

Outside, Stefan coughed. "Good morning, my love. I hope you slept well?"

Synol pursed her lips and placed a protective hand over her belly. Her face changed in a heartbeat from curious to calm. "I'm quite well, Stefan. I shall come join you for breakfast."

The two sisters eyed each other for a long moment, then took their respective seats while their minds whirled.

Ynya remembered the shoes her mother had packed for her. She noticed them deep in the hull when she was heading home. Mama knew Ynya's magic better than anyone, and she would have never made the mistake. Papa might have accidentally packed shoes for his daughter, but not Mama. Mama wouldn't have made such a minor mistake like that. She was too careful, too cautious, and her mind never stopped working. She would have never sent Ynya with shoes, so why did she insist on packing them?

Ynya needed to get away from this caravan and into town so she could find out what was in that boat.

She had an urge to ask Synol to see if the boat was still tethered at the dock, but wasn't willing to risk asking anything too specific with the nurse in the room.

So, Ynya closed her eyes and went over all her memories before she left, trying to recall every word her mother told

her, every word between her parents, and every single thing
loaded onto the boat.

Chapter Thirty

"Stefan, wait!" Synol called to her husband, who clomped outside on his horse.

"Yes, my love?"

"Come around here, please."

"Of course."

Synol wore a sour expression and shared a quick glance with Ynya as Stefan rode his horse from one side the carriage over to the other. After a few moments, Synol opened the carriage door, made sure he was there, and pointed to the ruined town.

"Did you have anything to do with this?" Synol's tone dripped with vitriol and accusation.

She sounded like Mama when she was mad.

Stefan recoiled. "Of course not, my love. I wasn't aware of anything happening with Marsfjord until the soldiers arrived with their accusations for your sister."

"Are you aware my mother was raped after she was stabbed? If my sister was accused of burning down this town, how could that have possibly happened?"

"Mama wasn't the only one," Ynya piped in. She kept her gaze pointed at the rear of the cabin, not wanting to look out the open doorway at the destruction. Her mind was a jumble of emotions and looking outside was sure to set them off.

Synol sucked in the cold air sharply. "So, there were multiple women killed and raped in the village. Does that sound like the work of a sixteen-year-old maiden?"

Stefan gulped and looked away from the carriage, but not at the town. "No, my love."

"Are you aware of any contract your father signed for me?"

"For you? You mean the marriage contract?"

"I'm talking about a contract between him and the Frost Queen, giving me over in marriage in exchange for knowledge of where my family was."

Stefan looked worried. "I'm sorry, my love. I know nothing about this."

"Then I ask you to do one thing for me."

"Anything, my love." Stefan gripped the reins tighter. The leather creaked in his hands.

"Go to your father, ask him about everything. Ask him if he made a deal with the Queen for my hand in marriage. Ask him if he gave the location of Marsfjord. Ask him if the queen sent her armies to murder everyone and set fire to my village."

Stefan's face paled, then flushed red. "I will, my love. I will go speak to him. I can assure you I was not aware of any contract, but I'm also of the understanding that the Frost Queen is a just ruler, and I'm sure we can work all these things out once we get to where we are going. I'm sure it's just a simple misunderstanding."

Synol breathed in, long and slow. She replied through clenched teeth. "Go talk to him and bring me your reply."

"Yes, my love."

Synol closed the door and buried her head in her hands.

"I don't believe him." Ynya said, still looking at the back of the cabin. As much as she'd tried to avoid getting into the middle of it, every response he gave just made her blood boil even more. "I'm sorry Synol, I don't mean to cause you grief, I just can't think of anything else right now."

Synol nodded. "I understand. I don't know what else to think right now, either."

"My lady?" It was the nurse, who barely spoke a word the entire time they'd been on the road.

Synol looked up.

"My lady, I'm so sorry. I didn't know."

Synol's face grew hard. "Didn't know what?"

"I have been telling Lord Torkelsen everything you two discussed."

"I figured as such. Do you know why he asked you to do that?"

Edith shook her head. "I did overhear him speaking with the woman in black last night. They discussed you."

"Me?" Synol was taken aback. "Why me? What was it about?"

"I only heard bits of the conversation, but he was furious that you were brought along on this trip. He said it wasn't part of the contract."

"I knew it," Ynya gritted her teeth.

"Quiet." Synol snapped. "Anything else?"

The nurse nodded. "If you have magic, then the Frost Queen will want you, so she has to get you tested."

Synol leaned back in her bench and sighed. "You were right, Ynya. You were right all along."

Ynya had waited years to hear her sister say these words. For years she'd dreamed of pointing and shouting that she was right. But those words were hollow in her mind. They were painful words, not words of love and understanding. They were fiery words.

"I'm sorry, Synol. I'm sorry for all of this. I'm sorry I wasn't there for your wedding. I'm sorry I wasn't there for Mama and Papa. I'm sorry I don't know where Finny and Meki are."

Synol stood in the small space and paced back and forth.

"My lady?" The nurse chimed in. "Is there something I can get you?"

Synol worked her fingers once again, like she was gearing up to punch something. It was a slow, methodical movement, like she was trying to prepare her fingers for something they haven't done in a long time.

"Synol?" Ynya finally had to ask. "What are you thinking?"

Synol stopped. "You need to get out of here."

Ynya's heart raced once again. "What? No, we need to go together."

"In the daylight? There are no fires, and I have no clothes to help me survive. It's how they keep me in here, or have you not noticed? They don't need chains for me, just lack of warm clothing. As much as I worry about my father-in-law and what he might have done to obtain me for his son, I at least have a powerful family with wealth that might have influence with the Frost Queen.

"They already did an adequate job of protecting me thus far. Maybe they can bribe guards or something, but I don't think they will do it for you. You need to run. Make it to the dock and jump into the water and swim. Hide somewhere no one else knows about. You know these hills and caves better than anyone else. They will never find you."

"But–"

"No!" Synol's eyes burned with determination. "I'm done sitting on the side and watching everyone else control my life. It's time I started making my own decisions. I'm telling you what to do for once, Ynya. You need to run."

She turned to Edith. "I'm going to need something from you, but it's going to be dangerous. I shouldn't ask you but I have no one else here."

"Anything, my lady. I should have never betrayed you like I did."

Synol nodded. "I understand, but for now, we need to get Ynya out of here."

Chapter Thirty-One

"Are you sure you won't come with me?" Ynya was beside herself, still underneath the blanket in case anyone else came into see them.

"I'm sure. You know I won't survive out there. Remember the 'demonstration' the woman gave last night? The risk of one of us getting hurt or killed goes up the more who try to run. I think this is the best course of action. I will survive while you go on ahead and try to find our sisters."

Ynya wanted to hug her sister so much right now. She wanted to take her in her arms and never let go. Part of her mind even wanted to just stay right here, see where this caravan was going. At least I'm with one of her sisters, right? And supposedly they were heading to the same place where her other sisters were being held.

"No, Ynya."

"What?"

"I see the look in your eye. You're scheming something, and I won't have it. All I have to do is yell, and any plans you are working on right now are gone. We've been over this. You run."

Ynya grumbled. "Fine, but I will find you as soon as I can."

Synol returned a sorrowful, but warm smile. "I expect you will. Are you ready?"

Ynya squared her mind, willing her heartbeat to slow to a comfortable rhythm. She needed to be calm for this next part.

The caravan made their way east now, just past the curve in the road that took them on to Lyraville. With Marsfjord to their rear, she would need to run as fast she could before they shot their arrows.

Synol was right. Any more delay and it was just farther she needed to run.

"Do it."

Synol gave her a sad frown. "I love you, Ynya. I haven't told you that enough."

"I love you, too."

With a nod, Synol stood and opened the door to her cabin, clutched one hand to her stomach, and yelled.

"Stefan! Where is the nurse? I think something is wrong!"

"What? Nurse? Father!"

Ynya screamed. "Help my sister!"

The horse reared back and whinnied, attracting the shouts of a few guards.

The door banged open farther, the woman in black was there, amazingly fast. She glanced at Ynya, who still huddled in the blanket in the corner. The two shared a look for a moment before she turned to Synol, placing a hand on her lower back. "Where are you hurt?"

The wagon lurched, throwing everyone into the air an inch or two, and Synol hit her head on the ceiling. "Ouch!"

"Damn roads," Nora muttered. "Stop the caravan!"

"Where is my nurse!" Synol yelled, one hand on her stomach.

The caravan slowed, but another lurch from the wagon sent Synol into Nora. The woman in black wasn't expecting the force with which Synol hit her. Both women careened out the door in front of Stefan's horse.

The door banged shut. Ynya was alone.

She threw off her blanket and dropped most of the chains she'd been holding onto for so long amidst the screaming and horse braying from the outside. She held onto one section in case she needed to use it as a swinging weapon.

She hoped Synol's gamble hadn't sent her under the horse, but the sounds coming from outside didn't sound like the women were in any real danger.

"Good job, Synol. I'll be back for you."

Ynya opened the door opposite the commotion and glanced out. The nurse ran up the side and gave her a nod. "I'm coming, I'm coming!" She turned in front of Stefan's horse and screamed, causing one of the two horses pulling the carriage to buck.

Any eyes still watching the road should have all turned to the drama playing out currently. It was time for Ynya to make her move.

She broke from the wagon and sprinted north, trying to put as much distance between her and the caravan in the opposite direction of where everyone should be looking.

All the energy poured into the previous night's activities had left her in an already weakened state, and the nurse had only been able to produce a small hardened biscuit to give her. It wasn't a lot, but as long as Ynya didn't have to fight or run too far, she should be all right.

Her previous time out here with the woman in white fur had told her that there were plenty of trees and rocky outcroppings in which to hide and slowly make her way to the coast. All she needed to do was make it to those rocks. By the time anyone noticed she was gone, they would waste too much time to find her. By then it would be nightfall.

Ynya's heart pounded steadily in her chest. Even the cool spot of magic her mother left her beat hard. Thoroughly exhausted, she dug deep to keep moving her legs, to keep running and not look back.

She came over a small rise and saw the rocks in the distance. A mile, maybe less.

A sharp object punctured clean through her leg. Screaming, Ynya tripped and fell face-first into the snow.

Through a haze of pain, Ynya saw the distinct shape of a black arrow embedded in the ground next to her, the nocking still glistening with red blood.

The woman in white had shot her.

Chapter Thirty-Two

Ynya rolled on her back and tried to get to her feet, but her wounded leg wouldn't respond. She tried again, and one of her bare toes wiggled slightly. What arrow would cause a single hit to prevent someone from even moving their entire leg?

Pink blood spread out on the snow below her as she concentrated on sending warmth down to her leg. She needed to keep moving.

Movement caught her eye and she looked up as the fur-clad woman stood above her, an evil grin on her face.

"You thought you could escape me in the middle of the day?"

"No," Ynya replied through gritted teeth. "I just needed to get you alone."

Ynya threw the red-hot chain she'd kept coiled around her hand at Kalda.

The woman in white raised her arm in defense. The burning chain wrapped around her hand twice before clanging together.

Kalda let out a terrifying scream and Ynya turned to run, forgetting about her leg. It was mostly numb now, but the pain shooting down into her toes told her that it was still functional.

"Move!" Ynya yelled at herself. She managed to get to a standing position, and glanced back at the caravan. No one was running out toward her location.

The woman in white continued to scream while she looked at her charred hand.

"Guess you won't be using that to shoot people anymore."

With pains shooting through her leg, she shuffled down the small slope to hide her bright red hair from the road.

Ynya had a mile to go to get to the rocks. Then she would be safer.

"Get back here, you bitch!"

Ynya turned around as Kalda came down the small rise. The chain was gone, as was the woman's hand. Left behind was a charred stump. A steady stream of blood dripped onto the snow with each step. Above the stump was the distinct mark of silver on her skin, similar to the woman in black.

Ynya's heart beat faster as the woman got closer.

There was no way she would make it to the rocks. No way to find a stream or food in this time.

Ynya stopped. Her only chance was to stand and fight.

She had nothing on her, but her stained dress and a useless leg. Her only weapon was in the snow, used up and unable to help her anymore.

Her magic was so low she barely felt it anymore, and she knew she needed to have some energy left in order to not freeze in the snow.

From behind her back, Kalda pulled a thin dagger like the one Nora wielded.

Ynya gulped. If both women were as fast with those as the other, all it would take is a single stab in the right location and Ynya would be on the ground unable to use what little magic she had left.

She pulled heat back from her leg, which was starting to tingle now, a good sign. She needed all the magic her body could spare.

An image flashed through her mind. A dark cave, two screaming girls. Claws and bright lights. Arguments.

The thing she and Synol never spoke about. The unpleasant time from her childhood had driven the two apart, but right now Ynya's survival was what mattered.

The hidden cave wasn't far from here. She hadn't explored it in so long, she didn't even know if the cave was there anymore. But it was hidden, safe, and might even have leftover, if disgusting, food.

Ynya didn't know if the bear was still there, but that threat would have to be dealt with later. For now she needed to handle the woman following her.

Memories of that fateful day flooded back into Ynya's mind. She'd fought the bear, and told Synol to run while she stayed.

Now, they had swapped roles, Synol fighting back at the camp to give her a chance to escape.

The memory sparked an idea.

Ynya wasn't helpless at all. She carried a weapon that had protected her for years.

An evil grin crossed her mouth as the woman in white squared off a few feet away.

"I'm going to enjoy gutting you, you little ingrate. You will pay for my hand."

Ynya concentrated on the blade. The woman only had one weapon and one good hand, so focusing on the blade seemed the most important.

In her chest, Ynya felt the steady, rhythmic strum of her heart. She was calm, she was collected. She was ready.

Ynya ran a hand between her hair, grabbing a long strand and yanking. She wound the thin fiber around the tips of her index fingers and held the ends in place with her thumbs.

She poured heat into that hair.

Between her fingers, her hair glowed a brilliant white, just like it had when she'd used this trick to light her way down the long underground tunnels littering the Razorclaws. She had used her hair to defend herself.

The difference this time, was how much heat she poured into her hair.

The illumination was so bright that it was nearly blinding in the mid-morning light.

Kalda hesitated, then lunged.

Having been struck by the blade many times before, Ynya knew the direction it was headed. Left thigh, right side, left shoulder.

Her vision wavered once again. Pouring so much energy into a strand of hair might take her below her ability to stay heated.

Kalda yelled as she lunged.

Ynya anticipated the blade and dodged.

Kalda was incredibly fast. The blade just missed Ynya's skin. It caught the fabric of her dress and tore a large slit through the bunched cloth.

Ynya released her hair from her left hand and snapped it with her other hand like a whip.

The tip of her white-hot hair wound around Kalda's already injured arm, burning through the leather gauntlets and slicing deep into her flesh.

Kalda stumbled, screaming out in pain.

Ynya kicked out with her good leg, pushing the woman to the side. Ynya fell to the snow in a heap, but rolled back to her feet faster than she thought she could.

In a heartbeat, Ynya grabbed another hair and poured more energy into it. She took a step back as Kalda scrambled to her feet.

Their gaze met and Kalda's eyes bore a ferocity Ynya hadn't seen in anything but wild animals. Her eyes were fierce, but she was confused how Ynya was still standing, still attacking.

Kalda was worried she would lose.

Ynya spat. "Nora attacks the same way you do. You're too predictable."

"And you're going to die."

Ynya ducked low and slid forward in the snow, whipping her second hair at the woman's leg, slicing deep into her thigh. The heat from her hair cauterized the wound, sending the aroma of burned flesh into the air.

Kalda stumbled, took a shaky step, then fell sideways into the snow. Still, she struggled to get up.

Ynya grabbed one more hair from her head, wound it around her fingertips and poured heat into it once more. She was wobbly, barely able to focus. Her vision failed. *This is it; the last strand.* She needed to end this now and get away from here.

Kalda got to her feet. She too was stumbling, unable to

use much of her left side, but her right side was still deadly with the knife.

Ynya needed to remove the knife from the equation.

Kalda hopped on one leg. Blood poured from the gash in her left thigh. She wouldn't last long, but even hopping, she covered more ground than Ynya.

The woman lunged.

Ynya tried to dodge, but she was too late. The knife pierced her shoulder. Heat from the wound flared for only a second before her entire body went cold.

No! My magic!

Ynya crumpled in a heap as the inner heat she relied on failed her. Her muscles lost all power, her magic disappeared from within her, and she fell.

Even half-damaged, the woman in white was a terrifying reminder of the power of the Frost Queen's army.

Kalda'd won. But she'd overextended in her attempt to make her one dagger thrust count.

Kalda hopped twice then ran into Ynya's falling form. Their bodies intertwined and fell on top of each other in a heap.

Ynya was on the bottom, her arms extended in front of her with the glowing hot hair between them. She'd never gotten the chance to use it.

Kalda fell, crushing Ynya.

But as she fell, Kalda's eyes went wide as she realized she'd fallen right on top of the red-hot fiber.

Ynya had already poured more energy into it than she had to spare, and a half-second after her magic snuffed out, the heated hair sliced through Kalda's left shoulder and lodged in her neck.

Kalda let out a momentary scream before it cut off and ended in a whimper.

All signs of life exited Kalda's eyes as her head came to rest inches away from Ynya's face.

Ynya stared horrified at the lifeless woman for a moment. She couldn't move, she couldn't yell. She couldn't do anything. She had no magic.

Cold seeped in from the tundra below as Ynya's injuries overwhelmed her delicate frame. Her enemy's residual body heat was the only thing keeping her warm.

As she faded into black, Ynya hoped that her sister hadn't gotten in too much trouble.

The last thing in Ynya's vision was the woman in white's dead eyes.

Ynya drifted off into the dark cold abyss of unconsciousness.

Chapter Thirty-Three

✿❧

Ynya dreamed of frost bears, par cooked beets, and battling on the frost plains.

She dreamed of Synol, and her husband, and regrets for things left unsaid.

She dreamed of her mother, trying to get her to wake up as she lay frozen in the snow in front of her house. Above her, a young woman with golden hair struggled to reach her, but lay frozen with an axe in her back. Her eyes pleaded for mercy, for answers. Behind her, a beautiful woman adorned in black feathers watched with rapt pleasure.

SHE WOKE UP COLD.

Ynya had never been so cold in her life. Even at her most magic-deprived as a young girl, she'd always managed to keep a bit back to ensure she produced enough body heat.

Even lying in the cell deprived of magic, she'd never been this cold.

One side of her body felt frozen to the hard ground, while the other side was warm and comfortable.

She shivered, trying to remember what had happened.

She had fought for her life.

Ynya was going to die. She was stabbed, but she managed to slice the woman in white open with her last hair, draining the last bits of her power.

Ynya relaxed. Now it all made sense. She lay on the ground, her final bits of residual unconscious heat had melted the snow to the bare earth. Atop her lay the woman in white fur.

Only...it wasn't. The furs the woman wore were different than what she looked at now. The woman had been lithe and muscular, but the form next to hers was large and soft.

A low rumbling sound reverberated through her chest, causing the hairs on her arms to raise in alarm.

It was terrifyingly dark.

There should be stars. Where are the stars or the moon? Where is the caravan, or the soldiers looking for me?

Ynya tensed, realizing her hand shook from the cold. Or was it fear?

She needed to see. She needed information to escape this situation. Slowly, Ynya raised her fingers to a strand of hair and poured a minuscule sliver of heat into it.

A tiny pinprick of white light, smaller than a candle, lit up the immediate area.

Ynya lay on a bare patch of ground covered with a thick coating of rough white particles that jabbed into her side and face.

The large form with the white fur moved, the rumbling low noise coinciding with the sudden shuddering movement.

Ynya tensed even more. She knew where she was. She had been here before and had barely escaped with her life.

She increased the light a tiny bit more. Beyond her immediate area, the rough white powder turned into thicker hunks of white and grey. Beyond them, the chunks became bone.

She was in a frost bear den.

She was in *his* den.

Yolphinir, the massive frost bear that terrorized this area of the Razorclaws breathed in again. His thick fur moved, partially covering Ynya once again and keeping her warm.

She was in an ice cave, carved out under a massive glacier, lying next to the largest frost bear known to man, and she had no energy to move.

Ynya was just about to let go of the light when something caught her eye. A glint of red and a tuft of fur mixed in with the endless sea of white bones.

She scanned the coagulated blood of Yolphinir's latest kill. Curiosity gave way to horror as she craned her neck to see over the pile of bones. It wasn't just any kill.

It was the woman in white.

Kalda.

Or what was left after Yolphinir had torn her bottom half from her top half to feast on for dinner.

Ynya swallowed, her mouth as dry as spring flurries. Her hands shook with fear and cold. She needed to find a way out of this place or she would be next when Yolphinir decided to wake and feast.

She let go of her hair and tried to think.

Ynya needed food to get energy. She hadn't burned much magic with her hair. Being warmed by the bear's massive form helped her body retain much of the heat that she would normally have to generate herself.

But the only food she had near her was...

No. She wouldn't even think of that. Yolphinir caught and ate fish when he didn't have other, bigger game. There had to be fish heads or tails around for her to find.

Slowly, she wiggled her toes, then her fingers, then the toes on her injured leg. Over the course of a couple minutes, she systematically went over every part of her body, checking to see what worked and what didn't.

Nothing was broken, thank the Gods Above, but every part of Ynya's body ached. Her leg had feeling once again, but it pained her with every flex.

The sleep had done her some good it seemed, but would it be enough to get away from the most dreaded northern predator?

At the bear's next breath, Ynya rolled from her back to her front.

She waited. Each movement mirrored a breath from the massive bear. She couldn't afford to wake him.

He breathed, she rolled.

Crunch.

Ynya rolled over some unbroken bones. She stopped all breathing in case the bear heard it, but he didn't rouse.

Ynya realized at his next breath that she couldn't keep rolling like this or it would land her on top of the dismembered body.

She would have to sit up and move.

Chapter Thirty-Four

At the next breath, she braced herself with her elbow. Ynya and the bear continued like this for a dozen more breaths. Each breath allowed her to shift her body slightly in the direction she needed to go.

She sat still and quiet.

She lit her hair once again, taking in her surroundings.

The cave looked a lot smaller than Ynya had remembered from when she was a child. The vast emptiness of the mysterious cave was now nothing more than a hollowed-out glacier. The bones scattered on the ground were a terrifying reminder of the bear's very real destructive force rather than an adventure of an eight-year-old.

The half-dozen cave entrances were still here, but the one that had caved in had been cleared of its rubble over the years, allowing Yolphinir to come and go.

Toward Marsfjord.

If she could make it down that tunnel, frozen fish awaited her at the end. There might be soldiers waiting for Ynya to come back, but at least she knew the area better than anyone else. She just needed strength and she could fight once more.

Ynya tried to swallow once again, but her mouth and throat were so dry she couldn't finish the action.

Water.

She was surrounded by frozen water.

All the walls were covered in matted bear fur from where Yolphinir scratched his shedding coat.

No wonder the cave stayed this warm, most of it was covered in a thick layer of white bear fur. If she could stand, up near the top was clear, unspoiled ice, just waiting to be melted down for water.

Ynya watched the massive sleeping bear for a while. His breaths came haggard and rough. He wheezed too, something she hadn't noticed until now.

Yolphinir must be getting old. He's starting to sound like Hvarf pulling his mule through the village.

She sighed, knowing she'd never hear the kind old man's voice again. But now was not the time to dwell on what was lost.

Ynya stood, each movement timed once again with the bear's labored breaths. Putting any weight on her bad leg shot sharp pains up her thigh and into her back.

She might have a broken foot or worse.

Ynya shuddered. She wanted her Mama, she needed to heal.

Finally standing, she dared a small light to look around.

No fish.

But she might be able to get water if she could melt a little bit at the top.

Ynya plucked a shorter hair from her head and held it a

couple inches just past her fingertips. Reaching up, she poured a small amount of heat into the strand.

As expected, the ice melted, but elation turned to disappointment as the water ran down the inside curve of the cave walls and behind the thick layer of fur.

This isn't going to work.

Ynya paused, realizing something in the room had changed.

The slow labored breathing had been replaced with an even, careful cadence.

Her hand shook, releasing the strand from her hand, plunging the space back into darkness. In the instant before the lights blinked out, she saw him.

The form of the massive frost bear Yolphinir sat a few feet away from her. His scarred face trained on her lithe form with the intensity of a predator.

His one good eye was the last thing she saw, and the impression the last bit of light left on her eyes was nothing short of terrifying.

What should I do? Should I run, or crumple to the ground?

The bear sniffed the air around her, searching.

Ynya took a hesitant step back, pain lancing though her left leg once again.

This time, the pain surprised her so much she whimpered.

Ynya felt the bear's hot breath directly in front of her.

She shut her mouth, lifting her chin up.

Two more hot, smelly breaths streamed through the darkness, brushing the matted hair off her trembling face.

Yolphinir stepped toward her. His massive paws crushed the bones on the ground with a terrifying crack.

All he had to do was reach out and crush her. One swipe would be all it took.

Something damp and hot bumped into Ynya.

His snout.

Chills ran up and down her spine and she took another hesitant step backward.

The wall of the cave stopped her, trapped Ynya between an ice wall and a frost bear.

Yolphinir snorted again, and fear took over.

Ynya didn't think or reason, she just reacted.

Every ounce of magic remaining flooded her mind. Anger at everything that had ever happened to her flashed to the surface. Terror and frustration wound together, pushing Ynya to the brink.

She screamed at the bear. "Go away and leave me alone! You will not eat me today!"

All Ynya's anger and frustration poured into her hair. The whole room was bathed in an intense white light as her hair glowed.

She met the bear's gaze.

Half of his face was burned, with hundreds of scarred lines running from the top of his head and down the left side of his face. His empty eye-socket was a black abyss compared to his one good eye.

Yolphinir trembled with terror at the bright light.

The same bright light that caused those scars, all those years ago.

He knew the glow. The bear knew the only creature in these wastelands who had bested him in combat.

Yolphinir took a step back, growling. He took another, and another. Soon he was backed up against the opposite wall like Ynya was backed against hers.

They stood for a long minute, staring at one another in the intense white light.

Three times, Yolphinir snarled and roared at her, but Ynya stood her ground.

Three times he swiped out at her into the void between them.

Three times, Ynya didn't move, didn't flinch.

The bear whined twice. Then Yolphinir turned and ran down one of the tunnels.

Unable to control herself anymore, Ynya let go of the heat from her hair and slumped to the ground, exhausted and completely drained of every drop of power.

Chapter Thirty-Five

Ynya slept once again, and dreamt about Synol. She dreamt about a gnarled and twisted monstrosity with horns and a mouth that opened wider than any bear's. It walked on all fours and teleported around the room like it rode the wind.

Ynya woke covered in sweat, breathing heavy and rough. She coughed for a solid minute, listened to the rattling in her lungs with each breath.

She sounded like the Yolphinir the frost bear.

Ynya tried to move but her body wouldn't work. None of her limbs responded. She was so drained of energy that everything refused to work.

She was so exhausted that her body had no energy to even warm her. She was going to die here now.

"Ynya?"

Echoes through her mind told her she was going crazy.

"Ynya?"

The echoes wouldn't leave her alone. She just wanted sleep, but her coughing refused to allow her to sleep.

"Ynya!"

Her eyes shot open. It was a real voice.

She tried to reply, tried to talk, but her mouth refused to move. Her lips trembled as she tried to huff out a response. Her breathing turned to spasms in her lungs once again.

"Ynya!"

She had to be hallucinating because she thought she saw her sister.

"Ynya, can you hear me?"

Behind Synol stood Stefan holding a torch, a morose expression on his face as he took in the bones and gore on the ground.

"Ynya, are you alright? I'm here, it's Synol, little sister. I'm here."

"Sssss." It was all Ynya was able to vocalize. It wasn't even a word, it was a sound.

"Trrr. Trrr." She tried to say.

"I have water."

Synol produced a water skin, and held it up to Ynya's mouth. A few drops hit her parched tongue and soaked in.

Then everything went black.

YNYA WOKE AGAIN. HER MOUTH WASN'T QUITE SO parched.

"Synol?"

"Stefan, the torch. I need to see her."

The light in the room moved up, illuminating the scene once again.

Synol's backlit form filled Ynya's vision. "I'm here Ynya. I'm here. I came for you."

Despite struggling and straining, Ynya could still only

move her eyes.

"You've lost so much energy. I've been feeding you half-mouthfuls of water, but you need food."

From her coat pocket, Synol produced a hard bread and broke off small hunks. "It's old, and dry, but should help. With a little water it should just disintegrate in your mouth and you can swallow."

"What is this place?" Stefan grimaced at the half-eaten body of the woman in white. He looked like he was going to throw up.

Ynya tried to talk but a stern look from Synol stopped her.

Synol fed her a small scrap then gave her a tiny sip of water. "Let it soak in. Don't try to chew."

She turned toward her husband. "A bear named Yolphinir lives here. Ynya and I came out here once as a child. I figured if she escaped she would come here."

"Bear?" Stefan looked around with the torch at all the entrances. "Where is the bear?"

"Ran away." Ynya managed to get out.

Stefan looked at her with a mixture of suspicion and disgust.

"It's all right, Stefan. I don't think the bear will come back with us all here. We're making too much noise, plus the torch. He is afraid of fire." She turned and winked at Ynya.

Ynya tried to laugh but that turned into another spasming coughing fit.

"I need to get you some medicine. Mama's supplies should be back at the village. I will get those once I get this food into you."

Ynya ate a dozen more bites of stale bread.

Stefan paced, looking down the various tunnels with his

torch.

"Why did you come for me? How did you get away?" Ynya was feeling slightly better, able to speak in full sentences, but still unable to move her arms or legs.

"After you escaped, Stefan and I confronted my father-in-law about what he had done. He admitted to everything, Ynya. The marriage, the contract, he even had it on him, showed us everything. He said he was going to make sure I was left alone. Now that I'm married, he would make sure that no one touched me. He didn't want to risk me or his grandbaby.

"After we got back from confronting him, Stefan told me we should run, too. He didn't trust his father anymore after all the lies. He wanted to go find you to make sure you were all right. We can run away together and start a new life, a safe life away from everyone.

"So, we left as soon as it turned night. The black witch came after us, nearly got me, but stabbed Stefan a few times. Still, we got away. After running and hiding for a couple hours, and not finding any evidence of you being in Marsfjord, I figured you might have come here, so I led Stefan into the cave and here we are."

Synol held up another hunk of bread. "Keep eating, Ynya. We need to get you better."

"Yes, eat," Stefan said. "We'll take care of you." He smiled, then looked down one of the tunnels once again. "You sure that bear won't come back?"

Ynya swallowed and huffed, this time with no cough. "Don't worry about the bear. He won't come back."

"Well, we should still hurry. I can't believe this place exists. It's a good thing Synol knew where to find you. We never would have known about this place without her."

Chapter Thirty-Six

Ynya finished the dried bread and water. After being famished for so long, it tasted better than anything she'd eaten in her entire life.

She napped for a short time again. When she woke, her mind raced while she relived her most recent events.

She couldn't stop thinking about Synol's and Stefan's escape.

Ynya had nearly died from the fight with the woman in white, and the only reason she'd lived was because Kalda had tripped and fallen on her superheated hair, killing herself in the process.

Kalda'd been relentless. All of the Skarmyord had been relentless.

So why had the woman in black only stabbed Stefan twice? Not only that, but why had Nora missed? One stab took away your ability to wield magic, another, your voice. Yet another prevented you from walking.

Ynya had seen Nora move. She was so fast it almost seemed she could teleport. A pregnant woman and a noble who took horses everywhere hardly seemed like formidable foes.

Something about their story is wrong.

Ynya opened her eyes. Synol lay on her side, eyes closed. Stefan was nowhere to be seen, but the torchlight bounced off the curved ice walls down one of the tubes leading to the surface.

Down the tube that led toward Marsfjord.

Ynya noticed markings on the ice wall. At first she thought they were claw marks from the bear, but a pile of bear fur on the floor told her otherwise.

Stefan was marking the tunnel back to Marsfjord.

Terror struck Ynya. Too many things don't add up here.

"Synol." Ynya whispered. She needed to rouse her sister without alerting Stefan. "Synol."

"Huh?" Synol woke, her eyes shooting awake. "Ynya, how are you–"

Ynya shushed her. "I think something is wrong with Stefan."

Synol's eyes widened, then concern, worry, and finally a fierce resolution flashed across her face in the dimly-lit cave.

"Why do you say that? He loves me. The baby. He's helping us."

"I fought with the white mage, Synol. She nearly killed me. If you two really were fighting the black mage, you would have died. She's too fast, and too deadly with her dagger. She never missed when she took me down. He shouldn't be walking right now. He should have crumpled to the ground immediately after she stabbed him."

Synol's eyes narrowed. "Ynya, listen."

"No, you listen, Synol. I know you want to think the best of him, but you know we've both been used this entire time.

Maybe he is clean. Maybe he didn't know about anything that was going on with his father, but the woman in black would have killed him in a heartbeat if she thought he was any sort of threat. She doesn't answer to his father, she answers to the Frost Queen. All I'm asking you to do is be careful."

Synol's eyes went wide, but not at Ynya. She focused farther through the cave.

Ynya realized the room was a brighter than it had been.

"Be careful of what, dear sister-in-law?"

Ynya turned. Stefan stood at the cave entrance. The torch lay on the ground and Stefan had his fur coat off.

He was a lot more muscular than Ynya had expected for a foppish nobleman.

"Be careful of my father? You think he's the only one with plans? You think he's the only one with power?"

Stefan took a step forward and held out his hand. "Synol, come here."

Synol shook her head. "I need to be by my sister."

He frowned, flexing his hands. For the first time Ynya noticed the old cuts and scrapes along the man's knuckles. He'd been in some fights.

Stefan pointed at the ground. His voice carried an edge. "I said come here, wife."

Synol tensed. "Just because we are married does not make me yours to command."

He grinned. "I think it does, and it's time you learned your place by my side. I have plans for you, and for your sister. It wasn't my father who made the deals with the Queen, it was me. His wealth only started to flow once I was old enough to learn numbers, but no one would do business with a young boy. So he was the face, and I was the brain. I was also the brawn, for anyone who got in our way."

Stefan cracked his knuckles.

"NOW GET OVER HERE, WIFE!"

Synol shook her head.

Ynya tried to pull up her magic, she tried to move her toes, her pained leg, but all she could move was her head. She was too weak to do anything to help.

Please, Mama. Please help us. Gods Above or Gods Below, hear my plea.

Stefan moved across the room. He was fast, but not nearly as fast as the woman in black. He was human fast. He grabbed Synol by the hair and yanked her to her feet.

"When I tell you to come here, you will come here like the obedient wife you are!"

Stefan tossed her against the wall.

Synol screamed as she sailed through the air. She went silent as she hit the wall and crumpled into a fetal position on the hard packed ground.

Ynya watched, helpless.

Stefan strode up to Synol and kicked her. He kicked her again, and again.

Each time, Synol's breathless cry was cut off by his boot to her midsection.

Each time Ynya felt the sickening blow as Synol took her husband's abuse.

Ynya tried to heat up, she tried to pull forth any energy she could muster, but nothing came.

The only thing she felt was the steady strum strum strum of her heartbeat as she watched her sister get beaten.

"Please, Stefan. I will do anything." Synol finally managed, still crumpled on the floor.

"Anything? You barely do anything I ask already. How can I trust you will do anything for me? How about I make sure you never forget your lesson. It's the only way to trust the words that come from your mouth in the future."

Stefan reached down and grabbed her coat, ripping it off Synol and tossing it across the room. "How about I let you freeze in here for a while to learn your lesson?

He punched her in the side.

Chapter Thirty-Seven

Ynya cried, furious she couldn't do anything to help her sister.

Synol lay in a heap, still breathing, but unmoving.

Stefan stormed over to Ynya. "You have no idea how long I have been planning my marriage to her. For years, my father and I had to watch while she and your father showed up to town to sell fish. Years, I pined for her, tried to talk to her, but she never spoke back. Or worse, your bastard of a father told me to 'run home, son'.

"So, I had them followed, back to your precious town, to find out where she came from. And I changed myself. Started working on the ships with the sailors so I gained muscles and sea legs. If she wanted someone who worked on the ships like her father, then I was going to give it to her."

Stefan grabbed Ynya and pulled her to her feet, holding her at eye level.

"So imagine my surprise when the Frost Queen's soldiers come into town announcing rewards for the capture of four girls with the last name of Oblique. Do you know how many families in this area have the surname of Oblique? None!"

He tossed Ynya to the side.

Ynya fell hard, her forehead hitting a bone that cracked under the force. Hot blood welled and streamed down the side of her head.

"Did you know your father took your mother's surname when they married? I bet you didn't. That little fact took a lot of digging, and a little bit of torturing."

Ynya looked up at her sister. Synol lay on her side, clutching her stomach, sobbing. Blood pooled on her skirt. "There's something wrong with the baby! Stefan, what have you done?"

Stefan pulled some rope from his pack and bound Ynya's hands.

He paused tying up Ynya to look at his wife. "Don't worry, honey, we can make another baby. That one wasn't conceived on the correct night anyway. You must bear me a son first."

Stefan yanked hard, pulling Ynya's shoulder back at a painful angle.

Ynya cried out from the pain.

Stefan punched her in the side. "I better not get any trouble from you on the way back."

The two sisters stared at each other through sobbing tears. Ynya mouthed how sorry she was.

Synol nodded, frowning. She mouthed "me too," in reply.

"Everything was going perfectly. Soldiers were supposed to come and take all of you, but apparently, they can't even do that right. Now I have to hand you over and tell them

Synol was killed by the bear in order to get her onto a boat and hide her away."

He yanked Ynya to her feet, but she couldn't stand. She crumpled to the ground once again. Pain lanced through her side as her hip hit a rock.

Stefan kicked her. "Am I going to have to drag you all the way back?"

He turned to Synol. "On your feet! You're going to carry your sister back down the tunnel." When she didn't move, he screamed at her, balling his fist. "I SAID GET UP!"

Synol slowly stood, her body trembling. Her focused, concentrated stare never left her husband's. She flexed her hand over and over like she'd done earlier in the carriage.

Ynya saw the motion. Did Stefan break her hand? No, Synol moved it that way on purpose.

The blood on Synol's skirt slowly dripped down between her legs, pooling on the ground and staining the bones a deep crimson red.

Finally, Synol spoke. Her voice was eerily calm for having been kicked so many times. She locked gazes with Ynya.

"I'm so sorry for what I've put you through, and I'm sorry I haven't been listening to you this whole time. You were right. I should have seen the signs sooner."

Stefan shoved Ynya forward with his boot. "I'm glad we're all in agreement. Now grab her and let's get moving."

"I don't think so, Stefan."

He whirled on her.

"You...you don't think so? Did I not demonstrate what will happen if you don't do what I say?"

Synol didn't move, didn't waver, didn't tremble. She looked solid, immovable, like she was made of stone.

Finally, she pursed her lips. "You are right, my husband. You are sorry about the baby, but you were wrong about me having another son."

He chuckled. "And how is that?"

"It will be hard for you to fuck me when you are dead."

Synol threw her hands out, her fists clenched and knuckles white.

The ground around them trembled.

Ynya looked around at the tunnels for signs of the bear, but there were none. Then she felt the tug of magic in the cave. Instead of the fiery river that flowed through her heart, it was a rocky, stony river.

And it flowed from her sister.

Stefan's eyes went wide. "What is going on?"

"You are done harming anyone, Stefan."

A long, jagged rock shot from the ground, puncturing Stefan in his right thigh, connecting him to the ground.

"You are done scheming, Stefan."

Another rock shot from the ground behind him, stabbing through his shoulder, pinning him between two long rock shards.

Screaming, Stefan looked between the two sisters, trying to figure out where the magic came from.

"You are done harming girls, Stefan. I heard the whispers of the maids, and I know what you made them do."

Another rock shot from the ground, up Stefan's free leg, impossibly curling around his hips, and finally puncturing him between his legs.

Blood poured out of his pants leg, splashed the bare ground below.

Stefan sobbed. His eyes rolled wildly. "Please stop this, my love."

"You never loved me. You loved the idea of me."

Synol turned her hands, and the ground beneath Stefan opened up. The three shards of rocks, like golem arms, dragged Stefan into the ground, stopping when his head was about level with the earth.

Synol twisted her hands once again and the earth closed up around Stefan, trapping him with just his head sticking above it.

He screamed. Tears flowed down his face. He tried to move but the packed ground was solid around him, looking like it hadn't been disturbed in ages.

"Yolphinir won't stay away forever. I'm sure he'll be back eventually and will be hungry, so you be a good boy and stay right here."

Stefan screamed while Synol gently picked up Ynya and carried her part-way down the tunnel leading back to Marsfjord.

Stefan screamed as Synol sealed up the opening behind them with yards of dirt. Enough that the bear wouldn't be able to get through anytime soon.

Stefan screamed as Synol picked up Ynya once again and carried her through the tunnel.

And then, Stefan screamed no more.

Chapter Thirty-Eight

❧❧❧

Synol carried Ynya in silence. Ynya clutched the torch, holding a fire that for once wasn't hers.

When they were about halfway back to town, Synol placed her down, gently leaning her against the tunnel wall.

Ynya burned with questions, but she also burned with love and admiration for the strength her sister had shown in the face of such peril.

Still, the silence was comfortable, unlike the silence they'd gone through last time the two were in this passage.

Using her magic, Synol opened the earth beneath the cave once again. Instead of a gaping maw, she pulled up just a few square feet of rich, earthy-smelling soil.

After long last, Synol spoke.

"I'm sorry I never told you. Mama insisted I keep my magic hidden from everyone. She told me it was too dangerous for anyone to know about us in town."

Synol pulled a small paper envelope from her bloodied skirt pocket and held it in her hand. She gave it a shake. It sounded like a baby rattle.

"It was too difficult with you, however. You couldn't wear the same clothes as everyone or you would overheat. You cooked fish with your hands and boiled water around you when you willed it. You started fires simply by touching things. You were too outgoing, so Mama was forced to embrace it.

"She raised you differently because you needed it. You wouldn't be who you are today if you had spent your life hiding your gifts from the world. You were fire, you were bright. You couldn't be contained."

Synol unfolded the small paper pouch and poured a handful of seeds out into her hand. There were at least a dozen varieties. She moved them around slowly with her thumb, like she was counting them. In a sure and steady motion, she scattered them across the patch of earth and gently tamped them down into the rich soil.

"It wasn't just Mama's greenhouse that made her vegetables grow year-round." A surge of magic filled the area.

Green sprouts poked out of the ground, working their way to the sky in seconds rather than days.

Ynya's breath caught in her throat as she watched the plants grow so quickly. So much of her childhood, and the mystery of her mother's magic made sense now.

Synol chuckled. "I bet her garden didn't do so well once I left?"

Ynya shook her head, not trusting her voice.

Synol nodded, a serene and sad expression on her face. "I'm sorry I wasn't there for Mama and Papa. I might have been able to keep them safe. Build a wall around them, or bury the soldiers before they got into the village."

The sprouts matured into full plants, their leaves

reaching for the light of the torch. Synol waved her hand over them as they sprouted flowers.

One by one, she brushed her hands against the flowers. "Pollen, and bees. It's the only thing I can't provide with magic."

The flowers shriveled, and small fruits formed in their place.

Synol took Ynya's hand. "I hated you for so long because you were allowed to show your gift and I wasn't. I didn't understand what Mama meant when she told me how dangerous it was for us to be seen. I didn't allow myself to feel empathy for your situation. You couldn't control it, you couldn't hide it if you wanted to live."

Synol sighed and rubbed Ynya's hands back and forth, building heat with friction.

Ynya hadn't realized how cold she was until now. She was frigid, but she'd been so focused on her sister that she hadn't realized her energy reserves had completely run out a long time ago. She was freezing to death.

Synol continued. "I'm sorry you had to go through what you did by yourself. I should have been there when you found the village destroyed. I shouldn't have left. And I should have gone with you when you first came for me."

Synol looked back down the tunnel to where Stefan lay buried in the ground. "I wish I would have seen him for what he was sooner. I just..."

"You felt cheated that you couldn't show your magic. You wanted a family that loved you in your entirety," Ynya whispered.

Synol nodded, tears flooding her eyes. She wiped them away and turned, plucking a ripe strawberry from a plant. She put it up to Ynya's lips.

"Bite, sister. I have everything here you need to regain your strength. You are correct, I thought I needed a new family, but I understand now, I had all the family I needed right there in Marsfjord."

Synol smiled as Ynya took the first bite. "Eat, then we're going to get our sisters back."

Chapter Thirty-Nine

T hey crept up over the small rise, looking down on the campsite below.

Anger rose in Ynya's head again at the caravan she'd spent so much time trying to escape.

"Hold your fire in for now, sister. We are not ready."

Ynya barely contained her rage. They had spent all night slowly circling the campsite, staying far enough out of reach that the soldiers didn't know they were there, but close enough to make sure they accounted for everyone.

Stefan's father was there, seldom leaving the carriage and sulking when he did. Ynya remembered him taking those coins from Captain Nora. He still needed to pay for his crimes.

Ynya accounted for all the soldiers but one. She imagined he must have ridden north to scout out where Synol and Stefan had disappeared.

Three days and no one has returned. Stefan's father must be sick with worry. Good.

The woman in black was also gone. Ynya didn't know if

she stayed in one of the wagons all day or if she was able to teleport from a nearby town so fast that she didn't bother sticking around.

Either way they had most, but not all, of the people who had wronged them.

The remaining prisoners still huddled in a single wagon. They hadn't been fed for a day, but Synol had produced so many extra fruits and vegetables for healing up Ynya that she would be able to feed them all for a week.

Ynya was sick of vegetables. She needed meat. She wanted to cook some fish, but the prisoners came first.

Vengeance for her family came first.

"So you are telling me that you can sense things underground?" Ynya asked Synol.

"By touching the ground, yes."

"And you say there is flammable gas underneath Marsfjord?"

Synol smiled, a wicked, cocky smile.

Ynya hadn't gotten used to this new self-confidant Synol yet. The two had so much to catch up on, so much sister talk that hadn't been said in eight years. But they also had a mission to complete between the two of them. They both had to get back their sisters to fulfill a promise to their Mama.

"Don't worry," Synol said. "When you get down there, it will be so flammable that nothing will escape. You just promise me you won't be hurt by the flames."

It was Ynya's turn to flash her cocky grin. "You know I won't."

Synol frowned. "This isn't as simple as a wood fire, Ynya. I can sense the amount of energy contained in the gas down there. It's going to create a fire unlike any you've ever seen."

Ynya grimaced. "I think I can handle it."

"Give me a minute after I raise the walls, then you can ignite. Hopefully, you will know when enough gas is in there."

Ynya hugged her sister before leaving. She skirted around the camp about a quarter of a mile, until she was on the southern road. She stopped hiding and marched openly toward the camp.

It felt odd walking directly back into camp in broad daylight, but it was the best way to make sure Synol could see where everyone was.

"I think I see the red-haired mage!"

"Alarm!"

"To the south, on the road there!"

Soldiers grabbed Ynya and hauled her back into camp.

Stefan's father came out. He rushed up and grabbed Ynya's dress. His bloodshot eyes told Ynya everything she needed to know about how the camp was functioning.

"Where is he? Where is my son?" Stefan's father slapped her.

Ynya felt the rage build beneath her skin, but she kept it in check. She needed to stay calm for now. There would be plenty of time for anger and fire later.

"He is dead."

The man's face went beet red. "What? Where? How?"

"He was eaten by a frost bear. He thought that he could fight the bear with both arms pinned behind his back."

Ynya grinned at her joke. It wasn't very funny, but it was so satisfying to say it.

Fury rose in the man's eyes. He reared back and slapped Ynya again.

"I want him found!"

"Oh, you won't find him. I'm the only one who can make it there, and you have been rather rude with me, so I don't think I'll be doing much of anything for you."

Ynya practically felt the heat of rage off his skin, and for the briefest of seconds, she wondered if he were a fire mage, too.

He grabbed her by her dirty dress and pulled her close. "I will hand you over to the soldiers and they can do whatever they want with you."

She smiled. "That's fine. They know the consequences if they try to do anything. I can make any part of my body red hot." She leaned closer to the guard on her right-hand side. "Any part."

Ynya cackled, trying to sound as crazy as she probably looked.

Anytime now.

She straightened up as though she were in charge of the camp. In a way, she was. "I want to know if the prisoners are all right."

He slapped her again. "Why do you care about them? You should be worried about where your sister and my son are. There will be hell to pay–"

"Hell? Hell, you say? After what you have done to these poor orphaned children? After what you put my sister through with your tyrannical son?"

His eyes went wide and he took a step back.

"Oh yes, I know all about him manipulating you and everyone else around him. I know everything he's done, because we tortured it all out of him before we fed him to the frost bear."

Come on, Synol, where are you?

"He cried, did you know that? Your precious son cried like a baby ."

We're going to need to learn to coordinate better.

Losing what little patience she had left, Ynya turned and yelled.

"Anytime now!"

The rumbling started.

All around Ynya, the soldiers looked at their feet in wonder.

"Oh, did I tell you? Synol is an earth mage, and she's going to kill you all."

Huge slabs of rock rose all around them, three feet thick and five feet wide. They shot out of the ground one after another in a line, winding around the entire campsite, creating an impenetrable barrier in less than a minute. Men flung themselves at the growing stone pillars, but they were too massive to budge.

Even Ynya, who could melt metal with her bare hands, stood speechless at the sheer awesomeness of her sister. She'd seen Synol grow full plants in minutes and kill her abusive husband, but she'd never known Synol had been walking around with such immense power.

The placing was impeccable too, each pillar completely sealed with the next one, not allowing even sunlight to escape.

The ground stopped rumbling for a moment. Everything went silent, but for the men crying and screaming for help.

One soldier tried to climb a pillar. He made it halfway up before the stone jerked and threw him off. He now lay in a heap on the ground crying, his leg bent at a bad angle.

More rumbling, and the massive pillars leaned in and covered much of the sky, plunging the camp into darkness.

Even Ynya worried.

The ground shook yet again. Around the wagon full of prisoners, another series of rocks sprouted out of the ground, this time at an acute angle. Soon, the entire wagon full of orphans and the woman named Miss-Miss was sealed off from the trap Synol had laid.

After another rumble, the gas poured in through cracks in the earth like rising mist. Soldiers fumbled around, not knowing where to run.

The heavy gas clung to the ground, pooling around Ynya's ankles as she counted to sixty and gazed at Synol's stunned father-in-law.

"Synol wishes you the best."

Ynya held her breath. Despite her ability to withstand fire, she didn't want to put that to the test inside her lungs.

She snapped her fingers.

Chapter Forty

The world exploded all around Ynya.

Fire raged in a torrent, hotter than Ynya had ever known. It whirled and eddied. It was like the ocean, but more violent, raging like the worst hurricanes she'd ever experienced.

The fire burned every solider, every wagon, every horse and pack animal. Everything burned.

Even Ynya's dress.

She blushed. She hadn't thought about that.

Finally, the earth rumbled as loose dirt rose and extinguished the flames. The outer walls came down.

Nearly spent, Synol trudged up to the site, huffing with exertion. She still wore her bloodied dress and a half-burned fur jacket Ynya had managed to find in Marsfjord.

Synol stopped about a dozen yards away and pursed her lips to a line when she saw her sister.

Ynya tried to cover herself, but then gave up and threw her hands up. "Did you bring me another dress?"

Synol burst out laughing, then nodded.

Ynya walked over to her, feeling self-conscious, despite no one else being around.

Finally, Synol caught her breath and produced a plain white dress from her pack.

It fit Ynya perfectly, and was thin enough she wouldn't overheat.

"You're too thin, Ynya. What man would want a skinny little thing like you?"

Ynya punched her sister in her arm.

"Just let them out."

TERRIFIED BUT OTHERWISE UNHARMED BY THE FIRE, the prisoners stumbled out of the wagon. Synol distributed fruit while Ynya cooked all the vegetables with her bare hands like a griddle.

After everyone had eaten their fill, Ynya and Synol walked the grounds, looking for anything they could salvage from the fire. A few slightly-melted gold rings, the metal bits and shoes used on the horses, and the charred bones of the soldiers were all they could find amid the ashes.

They found no signs of the mage in black. This troubled the sisters deeply.

After handing over the gold rings to Miss-Miss, Ynya ensured everyone waited at a safe distance while Synol buried everything under fresh dirt, reshaping the land to match the road on either side.

Before long, it looked exactly as it did during summer. After another winter storm, snow would cover it up and no one would ever be the wiser.

. . .

THE SISTERS SPENT THE NEXT FEW DAYS IN MARSFJORD, showing Miss-Miss and her surrogate children where everything was in town. With Synol's help, they all buried the dead on a flat piece of ground to the north. Synol pulled a massive chunk of beautiful white marble out of the ground to construct a simple but elegant mausoleum for their parents.

Over the next days, everyone did what they could to make repairs to the village. Ynya heated glass out of sand to replace the panes destroyed in the attack on Marsfjord. Miss-Miss approached Ynya and Synol as they finished installing the last window. She placed a loving hand on Ynya's shoulder.

"You should have everything you need here, Miss-Miss. Thank you for everything you did. You kept me from making as many mistakes as I would have if I'd been by myself."

"You are welcome, my dear. We're a small, scrappy bunch, but we will survive. If your family could do it, we can rebuild Marsfjord."

Synol spoke. "Soldiers are going to be patrolling this area looking for us, as well as their lost men, so be extra careful for a while. We will spend a few days killing as many as we can, but in the meantime there is a complete basement I carved out under my parent's house. You all can hide down there if you need. Some of the older kids should stand watch along the road. Keep fires to a minimum and only at night until things become safe."

Miss-Miss hugged them. "Thank you, girls. I will do what I can to rebuild this town in honor of you and yours."

THAT NIGHT, YNYA DREAMED ABOUT HER MOTHER. SHE watched Synol and Mama hug and catch up on all the events that had happened since Synol left. They all cried over the lost baby.

Mama embraced Ynya in a huge hug. "I'm so proud of you, my little spitfire. You are growing and maturing."

Talia Oblique held her second daughter at arm's length and took her in. "It's about time, my love. It's about time."

Ynya could almost smell the earthy, crackling scent of her mother, like wet soil after a thunderstorm.

Almost.

Epilogue

Imryll Farora released Captain Nora Oblique.

The naked woman crumpled to the floor.

Imryll frowned. "Now look at what you've made me do, you've bloodied my floor."

Nora wisely didn't respond. She'd done enough damage from allowing the sisters to escape and destroy so many of her soldiers.

Imryll gestured to Khatar, who bowed and went to summon cleaning staff.

The Frost Queen walked back over to her window, looking out over the Fellsstav Valley.

"Do you know why I chose this location to be my headquarters?"

She leaned over the railing. The arctic wind whipped her silver hair in a frenzy above her slender head. It ran up her robe and sent chills down her spine in a way that felt like she belonged.

"I chose this spot because it's the spot directly north of where I will break through the Feond. It's also the northernmost spot of the Concordance. From here, I can see every-thing. I see my entire domain, and soon, very soon, I will be able to see farther. Once the barrier goes down and I take my place as the rightful heir to this land, I will rule this land as my race once did."

She spun, eyeing the crumpled woman on the floor.

"But I cannot do this alone, you understand. I must have soldiers who will work with me, not just for me. I need doers, not simply nodders. I have enough of those."

Khatar came back into the room and bowed.

"See what I'm talking about?"

The Frost Queen spun back around, pausing to fling a piece of skin out from under her nail.

"With me at the helm, the Concordance will bend to my will, freeze over, and eventually cover this entire land in ice. But I cannot do that without my soldiers taking the initiative they should."

Imryll snapped her fingers, and Captain Nora floated up into the air, her long black hair frozen to her face and back, still glistening red.

In the distance, the howling wind grew. Wind whipped in a frenzy around them, across the open balcony leading out to the vast space beyond.

A flurry of snow coagulated, born on the wind. A minia-ture cyclone of icy power.

Then it subsided. The snow and winds receded, and in its place was a massive spike of ice standing at least ten feet tall on the balcony.

Imryll floated Nora up to her face, two inches from each other. "You clearly haven't been trained properly, and must face the consequences. I think five days on the ice will be enough to remind you who you serve.

"After this I hope you will learn to complete the tasks given to you. After this you will be permitted to return to your post. But one more failure and I can make this last for decades. Centuries even."

With her left hand, Imryll gestured to the outside wall of the mountain. Dotting the frozen rock were half a dozen spikes just like this one. On each one was another naked man or woman, their mouths open in a perpetual scream drowned out by the constant howling winds.

Nora swallowed, not taking her gaze from the Frost Queen. She knew the fate of those that failed. She knew the fate of everyone in this country. She had made her choices and would suffer the consequences.

Imryll nodded and Nora rose into the air, floated over the spike of ice, then lowered down until the tip of the ice spike pierced her between her legs.

Nora bit her lip, trying to keep from showing how much pain it was. The howling wind plowed into her, sending hundreds of small ice spikes under her skin, her eyes, her nose; like being cut with a thousand tiny knives. Unseen power bound her hands and feet, holding her up but preventing movement.

Nora's breath came ragged and labored as she tried to withstand the pain from all sides, while her body weight slowly pushed an ice spike through her torso.

"Go ahead and scream if you like. You will eventually. They all do."

The Frost Queen turned away, then stopped, putting a finger into the air. She looked over her shoulder.

"You did say the sister had earth magic, right?"

Nora groaned, as close as she could come to affirming the Frost Queen's question.

Imryll turned around, a broad smile on her face. "This bodes well. Earth and Fire in one family. If the next two sisters possess the powers I think they do, this will be the only thing that keeps you from ending up a permanent trophy on the rock. It's just too bad you killed their mother. A mage able to produce children like this would have been better than any other magic you could have brought me."

Imryll blinked her eyes, and Nora slid down onto the spike an inch. She gave into the pain and screamed as her body began the slow process of tearing apart.

The Frost Queen shook her head. "It's too bad. All that magic, gone forever when it should have been mine."

∾

THE END

∾

I HOPE YOU ENJOYED THIS BOOK! IF YOU DID, PLEASE leave a review on Amazon or Goodreads. Reviews help others find my books, which means I can continue to write more like this!

Thank you so much for reading, and I hope you check out the next episode in The Frost Fervor Concordance!

- Tom Hansen

October 2018

Author's Notes

October 2018

What a wild ride this has been.

    I've never written anything so fast before, but once you know your story, and you have the characters in your head, it's hard to get it out fast enough.

The book started as a thought experiment for the origin of the Frost Queen, a character I was helping my wife do some backstory on for The Bound Concordance series. Before I knew it, I had a basic premise for what the Frost Queen was doing in the area, and that led me to think of someone who would stand up to her tyranny. I needed a folk legend, a hero for the people.

That led me to Ynya Oblique, the opposite of Imryll Farora.

Ynya is young, Imryll is old.

Ynya is fire, Imryll is frost.

Imryll would throw her own mother under the bus to get what she wants, Ynya will do anything to protect her family.

They were the perfect match, but I needed to have them spar. I needed a way to get them to fight one another.

So I had the Frost Queen kill Ynya's parents and kidnap her sisters. That singular event kicked off the events of this series, and I can't wait for you to see what I have in store for her with the next book.

I got a lot of feedback from beta readers that, other than Ynya, their favorite character was Synol. I have to agree. Synol's arc in this one was one of my favorite things I've ever written.

I got a major shiver up my spine, and may have shed a tear or two when I wrote her chapters. I love her so much. She represents so much of the women in my life: strong, feminine, stoic, caring, fierce, gentle, and do NOT mess with her family!

If you loved this book, I think you'll love the next one! Check out the preview I have in the next chapter.

One of the best ways to support me as an author is to leave a review on Amazon. Reviews help others find my books, which means I can continue to write more like this!

I realize Amazon does't make it easy to leave a review because you can't just hit stars and move on, but even a simple review like "Synol is the best!" goes a long to letting others know that this series is worth checking out.

Sharing the book with others on social media helps get the word out. So hop on the Twitters and the Instagrams. Shout from the top of the Facebooks and the Reddits that you love my story!

While you're out there on the cold internets, come say hi! I love to hear how my stories have entertained or touched you.

Finally, I have so many other stories to tell in this

universe, and I've already written one that I want to share with you. Anyone who signs up to my newsletter will receive a companion short story to this one. It's a fun little story I couldn't fit into the book so I'm giving it away!

Thank you so much for reading, and I'll see you next time!

- Tom Hansen

October 2018

Excerpt from Flaming Vengeance

BOOK TWO OF THE FROST FERVOR
CONCORDANCE

Ynya Oblique squinted as she waited for her sister's signal. It had been too long since they had made contact and Ynya was beginning to get worried.

She wished Synol had the same ability to flash her hair, but a flint and steel turned out to be an effective, albeit more noisy, alternative.

In the darkness, she monitored more than one form move about the small rise. Both road patrols wandered their posts, stamping their feet to try to keep out the cold and keep themselves awake.

A flash of light the next hill over caught her attention. A second later, the light flashed once again.

This time, Ynya focused on it. Synol's bright red hair and serious face was just visible against the dark night sky.

There she is.

It was about time. Ynya was getting tired. Lately, the soldiers had been posting so many sentries at night that wasn't until the sun was about to come up that the sisters were able to make their move.

Ynya had stopped counting out a delay two days ago.

None of it mattered, anyway. Synol wouldn't act until Ynya had gone down there anyway, so why bother counting to the second if you're still waiting on your partner to do the work?

That's probably good enough.

Ynya shrugged off her leather bag, noting the location next to the scraggly pine tree to the north of the camp. She put up the hood on her stolen soldier's uniform and buttoned up the front.

She looked in the bag, a gift from Miss-Miss who had insisted on giving her something smaller to carry things.

It turned out to be quite handy to have everything she needed right there. The cross-body strap held things securely and kept things conveniently at her hip instead of on her back.

She hated this part, the smelly clothes, the subterfuge, the idle chit chat as she pretended to be a soldier. She wished Synol would just do it, she was always better with the subtleties of language and knowing what to say.

I just want to blow shit up.

Ynya stood and jogged down slope to the soldier in the road. Given how cold things were out here and the constant howling of the wind from the east, she easily got within a few paces of him before he noticed her.

She raised her hand at him.

"It's your lucky day."

The soldier chuckled. "Oh yeah, how so?"

"Well," Ynya pulled the hood back on her large winter coat. "I'm here to save your life, but only if you can answer me one question."

His eyes widened, seeing her mass of curly red hair bounce out of the hood and catch in the wind.

He took a step back, still trying to process the sudden arrival of the largest threat to any soldier in the Hyndalskyr district.

He dropped to his knees. "I'll do whatever it takes, just please don't hurt me. I'm not a mage, I've never been to Reyoarfjell, I was just conscripted into the army and told that if I didn't do what they said, my wife and kids would be killed."

She stopped walking toward him and let her hands fall to her side. She smiled. "That is actually the answer I was looking for. Where are you from?"

"Laugar, to the south, Ma'am."

She chuckled, "Ma'am was what people called my mother."

"Sorry, Miss."

She frowned. "I'm not sure that's any better, but it is no matter. "Can you make it to Holmslatr on your own if you leave right now?"

He glanced toward the south-west. "Holmslatr? Isn't Lyraville–"

She shook her head, cutting him off. "Lyraville might not be around by tomorrow."

Horrified understanding swept across his face and his eyes went wide as he looked back toward the east. "I...I...yes, I can make it."

"What about the rest of the contingent? How many are loyal to the Frost Queen?"

"Just the captain and one other man, the big guy with the bald head. We call him The Cobbler."

Ynya nodded. "I suggest you head for Holmslatr now

and get to a safe distance, but wait for any other soldiers to catch up. Whatever you do, do not go to Marsfjord. Huddle up for warmth, make it to Holmslatr. If you arrive with your arms up and mention that you abandoned the army, you will be welcomed there, but your name and number will be logged in case we see you in the army again. You only get this one chance to return to your family."

He nodded. "Thank you, Ma'am."

"It's time for me to handle this Cobbler fella. You said big guy?"

"Yes, big guy, shaved head."

Ynya grunted.

She grabbed a single strand of hair from her head to hold between her fingers. She flashed three quick lights, followed by two more.

Synol replied a few seconds later with a spark from her flint.

"As you can see, we're more than prepared for this, so head on out and make sure to help anyone else that comes along here in about an hour."

With that, the man took off into the snow.

Check out Flaming Vengeance: Book Two in the Frost Fervor Concordance now!

About Tom Hansen

THE CREATIVE CURMUDGEON

FANTASTIC WORLDS. GET-OFF-MY-LAWN ATTITUDE.

Tom Hansen is the writer and lover of all things fantasy. While he can't seem to stick to a specific genre, you can rest assured that anything he writes will have that aspect of whimsy and world building that defines the fantasy genre.

His first series is the *End Gate Chronicles*, a modern-day urban fantasy following an older widow who discovers her own magic late in life.

His second series, *Enter the louVRe*, is set inside a video game, where an evil AI has trapped players and stolen their memories. Now, a lone minotaur must save the world from destruction if he has any hope to to unravel the plans of the architect of the game and escape unscathed.

His third series, *The Frost Fervor Concordance*, is set in a fantastical frozen wasteland, where a young fisher comes home to find her village burned and her parents killed. The fire-headed mage must track down her kidnapped sisters and battle the Frost Queen's tyranny in order to keep her sisters safe.

Tom lives in Arizona with his dear wife, four children, and two cats.

To follow Tom, check out his website or any of the link below:

www.scarhoof.com

- 📘 facebook.com/scarhoof
- 🐦 twitter.com/scarhoof
- ⓐ amazon.com/author/tomhansen
- **BB** bookbub.com/authors/tom-hansen-7a3f964c-dbe3-4b40-a702-f7c60c91c3b3
- ⓖ goodreads.com/scarhoof
- ▶ youtube.com/scarhoofplays
- ⓞ instagram.com/Scarhoof

Also by Tom Hansen

WWW.SCARHOOF.COM/ALSOBYTOMHANSEN

Adventure Fantasy

THE FROST FERVOR CONCORDANCE:

Inciting Vengeance (Prequel - Coming Spring 2019)

Igniting Vengeance

Flaming Vengeance

Blazing Vengeance

The Frost Fervor Concordance Trilogy (Books 1-3 plus bonus Novella! - Coming Spring 2019)

Sparking Vengeance (Coming Mid 2019)

Flaring Vengeance (Coming Mid 2019)

LitRPG/GameLit

ENTER THE louVRe SERIES:

Eloria's Beginning

Eloria's Calling (Coming 2019)

BECOMING DEATH SERIES:

Mightier Still

Urban Fantasy

END GATE SERIES:

A Moonlit Task

Mayhem in the Moonlight (Coming Early 2019)

Secrets of the Shadowed Moon (Coming Early 2019)

THE KORRIGAN CHRONICLES:

The Sacking of Gildebrand Manor

That Dammed Berehynia

Moloch's Twisted Menagerie

Freya's Wild Hunt

The Roswell Incident

Short Fiction/Anthologies

Ynya vs the Frost Bear: A Frost Fervor Concordance Prequel Short

Into the Void: A Steampunk Short Story

Glimpses: an Anthology of 16 Short Fantasy Stories

Futurism & Fantasia: Volume 1: First Chapters

Newsletter Exclusives

Miss-Miss's Near Miss (Adventure Fantasy)

Splashes of Wine (Urban Fantasy)

The Curious Case of Brendalynn Bobbins (LitRPG)

www.ingramcontent.com/pod-product-compliance
Lightning Source LLC
Chambersburg PA
CBHW020409180626
46812CB00003B/904